"Anne Pfeffer crafts an emotionally resonant journey from food addiction and binge eating to self-confidence and communal support. Highly recommended!"

—CHANTICLEER BOOK REVIEWS

"Sabrina and her upward trajectory [are] realistic, satisfying, and memorable all in one."

—MIDWEST BOOK REVIEW

"A truly memorable and heartfelt dive into the world of eating disorders and body positivity."

—HOLLYWOOD BOOK REVIEWS

"A powerful story about self-image, expectation, and the wounds we ultimately inflict on ourselves."

—SELF-PUBLISHING REVIEW

"Anne Pfeffer's inspiring, dramatic, and humorous novel *Binge* approaches difficult topics with tact, while each obstacle in the story reveals the strong female lead's strengths and weaknesses and teaches a powerful lesson about self-love. Pfeffer balances heartrending and humorous moments with sensitivity and ease."

—INDIEREADER

"*Binge* makes the reader react. Whether you want to cry with Sabrina or throttle her, it's a testament to Pfeffer's skill as a writer that she can evoke such a powerful response from her readers."

—PACIFIC BOOK REVIEW

"This story will resonate with readers who struggle with social pressure to be thin."

—THE U.S. REVIEW OF BOOKS

Happy reading!

Anne Pfeffer

binge

Anne Pfeffer

BOLD
PRINT
P·R·E·S·S

© 2022 Anne Pfeffer
Binge
First edition, January 2022

BOLD
PRINT
P·R·E·S·S

Bold Print Press
Los Angeles, CA
www.annepfefferbooks.com

Editing: Shayla Raquel, shaylaraquel.com
Cover Design & Interior Formatting: melindamartin.me

ISBN: 978-0-578-34629-8 (paperback)

Other Works by Anne

Any Other Night
The Wedding Cake Girl
Girls Love Travis Walker
Just Pru
What We Do for Love

To the people who made this book so much better:

Linzi Glass
Margaret Byrne
Mark Spencer
Shayla Raquel
Melinda Martin

One

I wanted to be alone with my Snickers bar. It waited for me, calling to me from its secret hiding place in the handy food drawer of my desk here at work. I needed it.

Now.

So what if my overfull stomach rolled like a ship in a hurricane, or I wanted to barf from that pizza I'd eaten for breakfast. When I was finally alone, I would rush to my drawer. I would take out my Snickers and let it talk to me. With its homely, bumpy chocolate exterior, it wasn't much to look at, but inside! I loved that chewy nougat-and-caramel center almost as much as I hated it.

All this, and more, I would experience as soon as I managed to pry my boss, Josh, from his office and send him swiftly on his way.

"Sabrina!" he brayed from his big armchair.

"Coming."

In a minute, he would leave to court a prospective client, a young actress on the verge of A-list status. Having fired her agent, she now toyed with a flock of them scrambling for her attention and seemed to be enjoying it all a bit too much. Which meant that Josh's tighty-whities were twisted into an even bigger knot than usual.

"I need that script!" he snapped. When meeting with a client over a script, he always liked to give them a hard copy.

1

I spoke in my sweetest voice. "Ask me nicely." If he snarled at me, I would throw it right back at him. I told myself it was no problem, that I was used to dealing with Josh, but still, my fingernails bit into the palms of my hands. *Hang in there.* Very soon, I would be in the soothing company of my Snickers.

Of course, the script was already in his briefcase, along with the contract he hoped Alexa Fredericks would sign at their lunch meeting today and a sterling silver picture frame engraved with the words WELCOME TO THE JOSH NEWMAN TALENT AGENCY. It had been my idea to insert an exclusive photo of a radiant Alexa receiving the Teen Choice Award just three nights earlier.

I got up from my desk in the reception area and entered his large corner office.

The floor-to-ceiling windows looked out over rows of emaciated palm trees that fringed the horizons of Los Angeles. It figured that, here in the land of the thin, even the trees were anorexic. The pale grays, blues, and greens of the office mimicked the colors of the city outside.

As usual, Josh had abandoned his massive marble desk for one of the armchairs grouped around a low oval table in the corner, where he liked to sit back and yell into the phone. On the wall above him hung what I thought of as The Shrine, a montage of various photos featuring Mrs. Josh as the willowy display wife—one, glamorous in red-carpet wear at the Oscars; another, standing bare-midriffed and dripping bling before an expanse of ocean; and a third, in a stunning vintage wedding gown, holding the arm of a youthful Josh.

Now forty, my boss still had that pink-cheeked baby face, which he tried to disguise with a sparse mustache and goatee. I was convinced his bluster and bravado were all part of his ongoing attempts to come across as more than twenty-five years old.

"The script's in your briefcase, ready to go," I told him. *Dead by Midnight* was by an unknown writer, also one of Josh's clients.

"Let's see it." He didn't bother to glance in my direction.

As I removed the script from the briefcase and handed it to him, I caught sight of myself in one of the many mirrors that hung in our office to allow our show-biz clients to check their appearance at frequent intervals.

This mirror covered an entire wall opposite an aquarium full of creepily drifting fish. The girl in the mirror had shoulder-length medium-brown hair that hung in limp strands. A face that was pretty, although plump and perfectly round. Ditto on the body. Shapely, feminine, but too much of it.

Josh practically vibrated with nerves. Without reading a word of the script, he tossed it onto the coffee table. One foot jiggled up and down while he cracked his neck a few times. "So, we all set?"

"I just confirmed your reservation at Rinaldo's of Beverly Hills. Twelve thirty." I faked enthusiasm. "I got you table six! You can't usually get that one on just two days' notice."

His face reddened. "I wanted table twelve! Or fifteen!" He needed to be seen today signing an up-and-coming starlet, announcing to the world that he, Josh Newman, was back—no longer a has-been.

"Six is a good table."

"It's a shit table!" he shouted.

"Not true," I replied evenly. "It's right in the line of vision as you enter." I knew because I'd driven to Rinaldo's myself to check it out and had the information stored in my copious JOSH—RESTAURANTS file.

"It better be," he harrumphed, but we both knew who'd won this round. *Point, Sabrina,* I told myself. He continued to grumble under his breath, but I ignored him.

It was time to move on—I knew that. I needed to fulfill my true destiny.

I was going to be a best-selling romance novelist. I still believed it, despite all my setbacks. Just out of college, I'd done temp work for three years while facing a tidal wave of *nos* and *I regret to says* from the publishing industry.

With student loans looming, I'd needed a real job and so began to work for Josh. It was to be a brief stint, and solely for the purpose of making more contacts in the book world.

Then, disaster. I signed with an agent who not only failed to sell my manuscript, but quit agenting after a year and a half to follow his calling as a white water rafting guide. I then spent months revising a story for an editor who was full of promises but was laid off before he could acquire my manuscript.

I was twenty-seven by now and still no closer to my goal. But, I assured myself, one day it would happen. I would publish and be able to stay home and write full time. I would find a way to pay my fifty thousand dollars in student loans. And to buy new tires for Lena's car. I groaned. At twenty-three, my little sister was an adult now, yet still always seemed to come to me for help.

Lord, I needed my chocolate fix. "You should leave now. I checked the traffic." I hadn't, but hey, it was always heavy in LA.

"I need you to pick up an anniversary gift for Corinne this afternoon."

Corinne? Did the enigma actually exist? If not for her photos and the fact that Josh called her often on a private line I'd been told not to answer, I'd have found it hard to believe. In the years I'd worked for him, I'd never once met my boss's wife.

I struggled to keep my face blank. "A gift? What is it?"

"It's at Phillipe's Creations. She and I saw it there." He pulled out his phone and texted me a photo of an exquisite diamond bracelet in a display case. "It'll be about . . ." Josh named a figure roughly equivalent to my living expenses for a month, or a few of his imported silk ties. "Take my platinum card. They're holding it for me."

I had to hand it to Josh. Every time I was just about to push him off an overpass, he would do something for Corinne that was so sweetly awesome that it almost made me like him.

"Oh, and while you're out, pick up my dry cleaning and get the Mercedes washed."

Did I say *almost*?

For the hundredth time, I wondered how Josh maintained his lifestyle with his modest stable of B- and C-list clients. Almost all his A-listers had abandoned him after his abrupt and embarrassing departure from Talent International. That had been before my time. When I hired on, he was already a one-man show, operating out of our little office and scrambling to get back on his feet. Three years later, he still hadn't made it out.

And neither had I.

By now in serious sugar withdrawal, I was about to boot him out the door. "All right, good luck!" I stood up, hoping he would do the same.

"Oh, and Sabrina . . ."

"Yes?"

A nervous half smile lingered at one corner of his mouth. "You know Rick's? This new gym across the street? I joined it."

"Cool." I wondered why he was telling me.

"They gave me some free guest passes, you know, for signing up. You want 'em?"

I tried to read his face. "Thanks for offering, Josh, but I don't think I'd use them." I had no intention of lying sweating on the floor, doing leg lifts while my boss watched.

He squirmed. "I mean, you're not bad-looking. Think about it . . . it might do you some good."

Had I heard him right? I knew I'd been gaining weight for a long time, a lot of it in the last six months. Heat worked its way up my neck toward my ears.

Right now, I was probably forty pounds overweight. No use kidding myself. On a five-foot-one-inch frame, that was a lot.

"*Excuse me?*" I wanted to stab myself, and maybe a couple of other people too. For example, Lena and her on-again, off-again druggie surfer boyfriend, Stuart Wadsworth Livingston III, otherwise known as Boomer. Anyone would get fat if they had to deal with those two.

Josh's eyes widened. "It was just a thought."

In my mind, his hair implants caught fire, affording me a moment of grim entertainment. "The restaurant told me Julia Roberts is there right now. You can catch her if you get going."

It worked. Josh grabbed his briefcase and raced off toward his Beemer—the convertible sports car was the "spare," the fun car that he used for dates and day trips with Corinne, or for work while I took his Mercedes sedan to be washed and serviced.

As the door shut behind him, I fell on the handle of my food drawer and yanked it open in search of my Snickers. It wasn't there.

I remembered now. I'd polished it off the day Josh called me an airhead in front of a client. It was supposedly for losing a letter that turned out to be in the pocket of his briefcase, exactly where I'd said it was. I had retaliated by accidentally dropping one of his two-hundred-dollar Cuban cigars down the toilet in the ladies' room. He'd been saving it for a special occasion. We tore his office apart looking for it, but it was never found.

My eyes burned from holding back tears. I tried to console myself with the thought of Josh rushing across town to see Julia. Good luck with that.

As I prepared to dash out, I took a quick peek into Josh's office to check that it looked okay. That's when I noticed the script on the coffee table.

"Unbelievable!" That was the big selling point for Alexa, the role that was supposed to catch her interest. Fricking Josh had left it behind.

This was exactly the sort of thing Josh did, and I knew it. Why hadn't I caught this? I must have been off my game.

I sprinted for my cell phone. *Josh,* I texted. *The manuscript is here. Do you want me to bring it to you right now? Or email it to Alexa?* I hit send, then waited impatiently for him to respond. When he didn't, I left to run his errands, taking with me the script, in case he called.

The first stop was Ralph's, where I loaded up on bakery cookies, Cheetos, and, yes, a Snickers bar, which I wolfed after paying for it in the checkout line, all the while muttering to myself about Josh. The nerve, suggesting that I was fat.

As I had his car washed and buffed, I contemplated keying its glossy doors and maybe running it over a curb or two. I picked up his Italian suits while resisting the urge to stage an accident with some bleach and a hedge trimmer.

At Philippe's, I picked up the spectacular gold bangle bracelet, set with a row of diamonds. I couldn't believe how expensive it was, but that was Josh. Stingy about a paper clip for the office, but willing to lay out the gross national product of a small nation to please his wife.

Having completed my tasks of personal servitude, I returned to my desk in the reception area, which, heaven forbid, featured another floor-to-ceiling mirrored wall. Ignoring my reflection, I made a selection from my restocked food drawer. Cheetos! They would keep me company for the rest of the afternoon.

When Josh unexpectedly swept into the office at four o'clock that day, I was sitting with my bare feet propped up in a chair, laptop on my legs, alternating between writing my latest novel and licking fluorescent orange Cheetos powder off my fingers.

"Josh! Hi!" He had never come back to the office after one of his lunches. In an instant, I was sitting properly at my desk, my bare toes and orange fingers hidden from view. I was about to ask how it went, but his dead, vacant expression stopped me.

"Can you believe she said she had to show the contract to her manager?"

The despair in Josh's voice made me suddenly feel sorry for him. "She'll sign. She just needs to run it by him."

Josh flushed red out to his temples and down his neck. "You don't get it. You have to strike while the iron is hot! You have to close the deal! That was my one chance."

I grasped at a straw. "You can still show her that manuscript. It'd be great for her!"

He paced back and forth before my desk. "I gotta do this. I gotta sign this client, Bree." The usual walls of superiority and judgment were crumbling around him. "I don't think you get how huge she's gonna be. She alone could double or triple our billings." But then he drew himself up. "And where was that damn script, anyway?"

My sympathy began to evaporate. "On the coffee table."

"You should have put it in my briefcase!"

"I did! You had me take it out. And you didn't answer my text." I felt like giving my wastebasket a kick, but that would have been childish.

Josh vanished into his office, leaving me fuming.

A ding announced the arrival of an email. With a jolt of excitement, I saw it was from one of the ten queries I'd sent out last November about my cherished manuscript, *The Passion of Cecily*. It featured a glamorous and spirited heroine, a pectorally gifted hero, and the prerequisite amount of seething sexual tension.

Was it possible? A glance gave me the answer. A New York literary agent did not feel enough of a connection with my book to warrant her further consideration. *I look for books that are truly special*, she wrote.

I punched the delete button. The likelihood of getting a positive answer from anyone else after all these months was down there with my discovering Big Foot or inventing calorie-free ice cream.

Josh appeared in the doorway of his office. I braced myself, but he was apparently done yelling at me, at least for now. Without a glance in my direction, he pulled his door shut and disappeared, leaving me to brood and lick the remaining orange powder off my fingers.

Two

I had fled the office by five and was home by six. Home to my soft bed with its squishy pillows, where my laptop would listen to my problems and a serving or two of Caramel Cone Häagen-Dazs would soothe me and tell me everything was going to be okay. I'd have a perfect evening of writing, content in the company of my characters, whom I loved as much as any real people I knew.

I hadn't loved anyone like that since college. A wave of nostalgia washed over me for my old boyfriend Mark, stopping the rhythmic spooning of my Häagen-Dazs. He'd been kind and fun, and he made me feel I belonged somewhere for the first time in my life.

Until that day in March of our senior year. We were walking from the Dartmouth campus to the little apartment we shared. Along our path, stubborn clumps of snow still clung to tree roots and window ledges, despite the efforts of the weak spring sunshine to melt them away.

Even in my down parka, I shivered a little, thinking how great it would be to go back to my hometown of LA after graduation. I was done with New England winters.

And Mark was coming with me. He'd been admitted to UCLA Law School.

"I won't miss this snow," I said. "You know, when we're in LA."

Mark stopped walking. "Oh, I've been meaning to tell you. I got into Yale too."

"Yale? When?"

"Last week." He scuffed the toe of his boot along the sidewalk, then peered at me over his glasses with those dark brown eyes that always undid me. I loved him so much. But his eyes were full of something that scared me, the same look I'd seen in my mother's eyes before she left us. A look that came from a great distance, as if—in her mind, at least—she was already gone.

"I wanna go, Sabrina. To Yale." He wasn't sounding me out. He was telling me. He was going to stay on the East Coast.

"Oh! Well, okay, that's a switch." My lips were trembling and my mind racing. "I guess I can do that. I can find a job in . . ." I tried to remember exactly where Yale was. "Near Yale."

"No. That's not what you want." Mark had pulled off his gloves and blew on his fingers to warm them. He reached out and tucked a strand of hair behind my ear.

"I want to be with you," I said, hating the small, pitiful sound of my voice.

"It's not going to work," he said gently. "We both need to move on, try other things."

Other things. That meant other places, other interests. Other girls.

He had wanted to stay friends, but I couldn't handle it. In the time since our breakup, I'd dated, but nothing had come close to the sweetness and fun of my first love with Mark.

I shook the sad thoughts out of my head, plumped up the pillows, and started back in on my latest project, *The Heartbreak of Cecily*. Its predecessor, *The Passion of Cecily*, was the manuscript that had been rejected today.

Heartbreak was the second in my series about Baroness Cecily von Staube, a beautiful championship equestrienne who saves a wild stallion from capture and wins the heart of the wealthy and dashing Count Richland. A third book, *Cecily's Lasting Love,* would complete the series.

I loved the impetuous, strong-willed Cecily and was convinced my story about her would sell. Eventually, a wise, farsighted agent would agree with me. For now, however, I would have to keep waiting. I set my spoon back in motion. At least I still had my Häagen-Dazs.

The next afternoon found me alone again in the office. My cell phone rang.

It was my little sister Lena, who had recently crashed on my sofa for six months after breaking up with that reprobate Boomer. Six months of weeping and nightly therapy sessions and unscheduled visits from the teary-eyed guy pronouncing his plans to "do better" and "make you love me again."

I'd been foolishly sucked into their tale of woe, coming home after working all day to make chicken soup and fling myself into the middle of their arguments. I called it "mediating." I took the results harder than they did. Forced to soothe myself with Tootsie Rolls and Cool Ranch Doritos, I'd increased my store of excess adipose by ten pounds. Meanwhile, Lena had lost ten.

She had finally moved out a month ago to a new apartment to be shared with her BFF from high school, Joanna. I hadn't seen Lena since, although I talked to her every day.

"So, what's happening?" I asked.

"Oh, you know, just wanted to find out how you were doing."

I could envision her, all round-eyed innocence, reclined on the sofa, idly extending one long leg. I raised an eyebrow. "Go on."

"Well, I've got a temp job lined up, but I won't get paid until next Friday . . ." She trailed off.

"And I need to know this because . . . ?"

I waited, thinking about the bag of potato chips in my food drawer.

"Aw, c'mon, Bree!" Lena became a little girl again. "Just a hundred dollars. To tide me over." She didn't even bother to promise she'd pay me back. We both knew she wouldn't.

We also both knew that I would somehow scrape up the money. It was a remnant of childhood: protecting and caring for Lena, no matter how hard it was. That said, I usually made her at least beg for it. Today, I didn't have the energy.

"Okay. But it'll be a check, not cash. And you'll have to wait twenty-four hours before you deposit it."

A beeping started. I didn't recognize the caller's number. I contemplated not answering it, but decided I would, just in case it was something important.

"I've got another call. Later!" I hung up, mentally pushing my credit card payment back for two weeks. "H'llo?"

A woman's voice. "Sabrina Hunter, please. This is Kaitlyn Mann from Fast Track Books."

My whole body flushed hot and cold. Fast Track was unusual—a publisher that dealt directly with authors instead of agents. Nine of my ten inquiries had gone to agents. The tenth had gone to Fast Track. "Oh . . . hi! That's me."

Was this a joke? It was 8:00 P.M. in New York.

Keeping one ear open to hear the woman, I wheeled my office chair over to my laptop and pulled up my query database.

Good thing I'd alphabetized it all while Josh and Corinne were in Bora Bora.

Fast Track . . . there it was. That's right, they were pretty B-list, as publishers went, but they'd been in business for twelve years. From what my spies in publishing said, they honored their contracts and were generally considered to be legit.

I had sent my query four months ago. To . . . I found it. Kaitlyn Mann, editorial director.

"Do you have a moment to talk?" Something in the woman's voice signaled excitement, promise, good things to come.

"Yes, of course." A strange light-headed euphoria misted through me.

"First, I wanted to tell you how much we loved, loved, loved your manuscript here at Fast Track! So much so that we want to make you an offer."

Had I heard her correctly? My brain turned in slow circles. This was the moment I'd waited for all my life.

"You want to publish my book?" I squeaked out the words.

"We do. You probably know that our practice is to acquire manuscripts a few at a time and to fast-track them, meaning that we push them through to publication in just three months. In your case, we'll begin production now and publish in July, in time for the American Romance Novelists Association conference."

Three months? I'd be a published author by my twenty-eighth birthday. But something was missing. I took a deep breath. "You realize this book is the first in a series of three?"

"Yes, but we think it will hold up well as a stand-alone book." Although Kaitlyn's tone was friendly, it had a kind of finality that made me close my mouth with a snap. "We'll see how it sells before we make any decisions about the other two."

"Okay." It would work out, I reassured myself. If all went well, in six months, Fast Track would be begging for the whole series.

"Our legal department will send you the contract tomorrow. We do ask you to adhere to a rather strict production and marketing schedule. That is, of course, if you're interested in proceeding."

"Oh, I am!"

"And we're offering an advance of four thousand dollars."

I clutched the phone. Four thousand dollars! All in one place at one time! *Keep your cool, Sabrina.*

"Check your email," Kaitlyn continued. "We like to offer our debut authors some marketing support in the form of an abbreviated author tour, or a day of promotional events. I've just sent you some really fun ideas for our marketing. Wait until you see them. You'll love them!"

"Thank you so much!" I made my voice calm, but inside I was thinking every dream I'd ever had was coming true.

Four thousand dollars!

The moment I hung up, I let out a shriek, then, trying to keep it quiet for the people in the neighboring suite, ran into Josh's office, where I jumped up and down. I called Lena's speed dial, but there was no answer, even though we'd just talked. Lena only took calls she was in the mood for. Unfazed, I whipped out a half dozen texts to friends, my thumbs a blur, then stopped for breath.

There had to be someone else I could tell. "I'm going to be a published author!" I announced to the ficus tree in the corner. "Thank you, thank you," I murmured, bowing to the fish eerily applauding me with their fins.

What did she say she was sending me? Marketing ideas? Cool! I pictured my name at the top of the best-seller list, lines of people around Barnes & Noble, me autographing books for adoring readers.

And four thousand dollars! I could put it toward my student loans, or I could, *omigod* . . . if the book sold, I could pay my debt off completely. I could quit my day job and say goodbye to Josh forever.

I'd be free!

Three

An hour later, I lay sprawled on my bed at home in my bra and panties, weeping and double-popping Hershey's Kisses. On my laptop, the screensaver had kicked in, hiding Kaitlyn's terrifying email. I would have read it again, but my eyes were all puffed up from crying. I checked the mirror on the closet door across from my bed—my nose was the color of a maraschino cherry.

Kaitlyn's email was only two paragraphs long, but life-destroying.

> *The whole time I was reading your manuscript, I was thinking of a certain photo on your website. You know, the one of you in that fabulous red beaded evening gown? It was just like the dress that your character Cecily wore in your book's dinner party scene, when she arrived on the arm of Count Richland. Since then, I've always thought that Cecily looked like you.*
>
> *I thought we could do an elegant launch party, and you could wear your dress and make a grand entrance down a flight of stairs, the way Cecily did! We may even find you a handsome escort to play the count!*

Red dress? Did she mean the one I got for seven dollars at a thrift shop? Back when I was pretty and skinny? The skintight dress that I couldn't slide my big toe into today, let alone make an entrance in? I'd worn it to a Halloween party, portraying a '40s Hollywood film star, then idiotically posted a photo on my website for the world to see.

In a panic, I pulled up my website and looked at the shot. Why had I posted it? Vanity, pure and simple. The red dress was hot and sparkly and made me look the same way.

Of course, Fast Track had checked out my website before making an offer. Publishers did that. *We'd like to build a whole marketing campaign around our glamorous author of glamorous books.*

Kill me. Put me down immediately, like a dying steer.

I reared my head back and eyed myself in the closet door mirror. Still had that back fat above the bra line. When I put my head down, my double chin loomed into sight.

My panic escalated into frenzy. *Kaitlyn Mann*, I muttered to myself. What did she look like? Hoping she was as plain as an old bucket, I went to the Fast Track website, then searched her name.

A face swam into view. A youthful mid-forties. Chin-length ash-blond hair, styled in an immaculate blowout. The cheekbones and sweet smile of a head cheerleader.

So unfair.

There was no help for it. I would have to confess to Kaitlyn that I'd ballooned, and she would have to ditch the red dress idea. The folks at Fast Track would be disappointed, but they'd live. They'd come up with a new concept that didn't require me to be something I wasn't.

Or would they? Were my weight and the red dress a required part of the deal? What if she canceled my contract—not because I couldn't write, but because I wasn't cute and marketable?

For that matter, what if Josh fired me for the same reason? Wasn't that what he'd implied the other day, that he didn't want a chubaholic at the reception desk?

Was it even legal for him to do that—to fire me for being fat? I was sure it wasn't, but what did it matter if there was no one around to stop him? I doubted the police would come after him for something like that. For me to sue him would take a lot of money that I didn't have.

Josh would get away with it, and I would begin a new career at the airport, driving baggage trucks.

As for Fast Track, I'd expected to do normal writer things for them—meet readers, speak to groups, sign books. I had not expected to make splashy entrances in small, slinky dresses. I was a writer, not a fashion model. The requirements were different.

Everyone knew writers were hermits. Writers didn't have to look good. They could be as fat as they wanted, since they were never around people. They didn't even have to groom themselves, if they didn't feel like it.

It was only right that there be some good jobs, some happy place in the world, for the unlovely. But no, here I was, totally screwed, because of my weight. They would cancel my contract, and I'd go back to Josh forever. Or until he got rid of me too.

Unless . . . It occurred to me that I had, after all, lost weight in the past—that once upon a time, I had dieted my way from total corpulence into wearing that dress. Hope flickered.

If I'd done it once, I could do it again. I rooted through the covers for my cell phone and calendar.

Forty pounds. Three months. That was about thirteen pounds a month. A little more than three a week.

I'd never actually lost weight that fast, but there was always a first time. I would make a commitment right here, right now.

I, Sabrina Hunter, would lose forty pounds by mid-July, wear my red beaded evening dress to the launch party of my debut novel, and float down a flight of stairs while hundreds watched in awe. I would be thin, fabulous, and a best-selling author—a person to envy.

It could be done. I was motivated. I was strong. I was determined.

My stomach growled, and I fell back on the bed, adjusting the waistband of my underwear.

I was hungry.

I'd lived for three days on cottage cheese and celery and gained a pound and a half. I was so hungry I could have eaten the glue stick in my desk drawer. During the same time, Kaitlyn, who never seemed to tire or sleep, had called me five times at work. Even though I kept my cell phone set to vibrate and had mastered the art of looking like I was working when I wasn't, this raised Josh's eyebrows.

I didn't need this new problem when he was already grumpy about Alexa and her failure so far to return a signed contract—or even a phone call.

When the phone rang again, I was relieved that it was one of the office lines. Josh kept lines one and two for his business, line three for himself and his wife only.

This call was on line two. I didn't recognize the caller's number. "Josh Newman Talent, how may I help you?"

Silence, then a woman's wavering voice. "Oh, I . . . I was looking for Josh."

"You've reached his office. May I ask who's calling?"

"Corinne Newman?" Her voice went up as if she herself questioned who she was.

"Hi! I'm Sabrina! Josh's assistant." The mysterious Mrs. Newman! "He's on another line. Should I tell him you're waiting?"

"I'm sorry." Her voice was so faint I had to press the receiver to my ear. "I must have called the wrong line by mistake." She seemed amazingly nice and normal, this woman who had inexplicably chosen to spend her life with Josh Newman.

"That's okay. I'd be happy to get him for you." An impulse overtook me. That incredible bracelet—I had to know how she'd liked it. "I saw your bracelet. Josh showed it to me before he gave it to you."

"My . . . what?" Her voice, if anything, became more uncertain.

"Th-The bracelet that he . . ." I felt a sudden horrible prickling along my scalp but didn't know how to stop. "That he bought for your anniversary . . . ?" What had he done with the bracelet? How did I know for sure he'd intended it for Corinne?

"I'm afraid I don't . . ."

How could I have blown it like this? I'd be fired before sundown.

Frantic, I opened and searched through my bulging holiday and birthday file, stuffed with key dates for my most important contacts, as well as Josh's. A lucky break: Corinne's birthday was two months from now. Time to improvise.

"I'm so sorry! I thought he'd gotten you the bracelet for your anniversary last week. But he obviously bought it early for your birthday. And now I've spoiled the surprise!"

"Oh, I see." She inhaled, as if for strength. "Well, you didn't mean any harm."

Did she really believe this load of bull manure I was serving up? I forged on. "No, but he'll be disappointed when he finds out."

"I won't tell him I know." Her voice warmed. "I don't want to disappoint him either. It was so nice of him to do that!"

"Yes, it was." *Grrr . . . That lying skunk.*

Josh's door flew open. "Here he is," I said into the phone. I looked up at him. "Your wife's on line two."

Wordlessly, he spun on his heel and disappeared back into his office, leaving me shaking. How could he? How could he give that bracelet to some other woman? And to involve me in his scuzzy doings! I'd even given the guy points for buying his wife something so beautiful. Now, to find this out!

It was five o'clock, and Josh was still hunkered down behind closed doors. I was done for the day, whether he was or not. I cleaned off my desk and stalked out of the office, trying to let the door close behind me with a dramatic slam. Unfortunately, the spring closed the door slowly, with a gentle woosh that didn't satisfy me at all.

That evening, Kaitlyn was on the phone with me again, despite it being nine o'clock in New York.

"We're putting a lot of resources behind this book," she said. "We believe in it, and in you."

You haven't seen me, I wanted to say. It should be enough that I'd written the book. But no, they wanted me to walk the runway for it.

"We'll need you to make a trip to New York in July," Kaitlyn said.

July! Josh had a huge premiere coming up that month—the latest in the detective/action series that starred our most important client, Buck Billingsley. This one was called *The Circus Murders*, and after poor ticket sales at his last two films, we needed it to be a huge hit. Josh would hemorrhage if I asked for time off.

I was still shaken up by the bracelet debacle. Who was paying for this trip, anyway? "I thought you guys did the publicity." I tried to keep the moan out of my voice.

"We do," Kaitlyn chirped. "But people want the author. They want to meet you and talk to you."

I wondered if there was a way to meet and talk to people without being seen. Like that singer who made her public appearances in a wig that covered her face. Except in my case, I'd have to cover my entire body, with a space blanket, maybe, or one of those shoji screens people use as room dividers.

The whole subject of clothing was hopeless. I'd been to New York, and I knew how those scrawny women dressed. I'd seen them walking down the street in the latest fashions, and I knew a caftan didn't take you very far on Park Avenue. The same went for giant ponchos.

"I have a job. I can't get away."

"I'm sure your boss will understand. I mean, it's not every day that someone launches a book." The undercurrent of steel in Kaitlyn's voice squelched any further protests on my part.

When the call ended, I tore through my closet, looking for any clothes I could possibly wear at public appearances in the Big Apple. It hurt to think that all those little dresses like the red one—which just a few years ago looked so pretty and revealed my cleavage and tiny waistline—had been replaced by long tunics, elastic waistbands, and dark, concealing fabric. Which reminded me of the shawl.

The shawl covers all.

It was my sacred wrap, which, once placed upon my body, was not removed until I was safe at home again behind closed doors. It had a bright exotic pattern and looked good with a black tank and slacks. And if someone wondered why I wore a wrap indoors, I'd just explain that I was cold, even though in fact I was broiling.

But where was it? Not in my third dresser drawer, its usual home. I rummaged through the other drawers, then checked to see if it was folded over a hanger. As the shawl kept failing to appear, a sneaking suspicion turned into certainty and then into anger.

Lena. She'd done it again. My one nice piece, the only thing I could wear, and she'd helped herself. She'd probably lost or ruined it, as she'd done with my sunglasses and my favorite sandals.

I suddenly remembered that I would be thin by July and therefore wouldn't need the shawl. Still, I should retrieve it before it disappeared completely. I placed a call and got her voicemail.

"Leen, I need my shawl back. Call me." I hung up. Among friends and family, we went by the nicknames Leen and Bree. We did it to avoid the use of our cutesy rhyming names, Lena and Sabrina, but it had always struck me as prophetic that her nickname evoked slenderness, while mine brought to mind a high-calorie, high-fat cheese.

I don't know what our parents were thinking when they named us. My mother was probably already plotting her escape. She left us just after Lena's fifth birthday and, like Mark, was never heard from again. As for my busy, distant father, he lived in LA but hadn't spoken to either me or Lena in months.

I tried not to think of any of them.

Four

I groaned under my breath as my stomach did a somersault. Starving, petrified that Corinne would rat me out on the bracelet, and too scared to tell Kaitlyn the truth about the red dress, I had lost all control and binged my way through the past four days. Just sitting down was painful, as it required me to fold my midsection in at the exact place where it most wanted to pop out.

Nonetheless, I still planned a headfirst dive into my food drawer as soon as Josh left.

"You have to go in five minutes," I called, shifting my weight in my chair. I'd been imagining that he was looking me over with an even more sour eye than usual. But he would never fire me. He couldn't. Over the last three years, I'd made myself indispensable. I liked to think I was the best assistant he'd ever had, not that he would admit it. Every day I handed him his schedule, every detail confirmed, every contingency considered. I caught mistakes, reminded him of people's names, made sure he was prepared.

But I was overweight, and that was hard for the world of Hollywood to forgive. Hard for me too. *Leave, Josh.* Like an avalanche, a binge was rolling in my direction, ready to sweep me up. I could feel it gathering momentum.

After he left today, it would be milk and Oreos. My stomach roiled in protest. *Please, no more sweets!* But my crazy mind, the mind that couldn't stop wanting, needing, craving comfort, would make me eat no matter what. It knew that Oreos, when soaked in milk, got really soft, so you could pack a lot of them into the empty nooks and crannies of even the fullest stomach. They were like ice cream in that way: they went down smooth and easy.

No sooner had the door closed behind Josh than I had my hand in the food drawer. I tore open the Oreo package, then shoved a dry Oreo in my mouth and chewed as I got the milk carton open. Cookies tumbled to the carpet, one of them even rolling away from me into the open reception area.

Oops, couldn't let that one go to waste. I went after it. Reaching for the cookie, I knelt and plucked it from the floor. Still on my knees, I was in the process of wedging it into my mouth when the door opened.

"I forgot my—" Josh stopped mid-sentence.

Our eyes met. The disgust on his face shriveled me into a cringing ball of shame. My cheeks puffed out like a chipmunk's, I tried to speak, but managed only to spray Oreo crumbs in his direction. Frantically, I chewed and swallowed, wanting to say something, anything to make this better.

"Save it," Josh snapped, his gaze like a blast of arctic air.

"Josh, listen, I—"

"No, you listen. I run a professional shop here. You represent me and the Josh Newman Talent Agency. Get up off the floor."

I was used to his quickly flung insults, his random explosions, but this . . . this string of carefully expressed sentences was infinitely more horrible. I tried to stand but couldn't seem to make my legs obey me.

"Pull yourself together, Sabrina. Fast. Or . . ." Leaving the unspoken threat hanging in the air, he turned on his heel and left without whatever it was he'd come back for.

My throat hurt so much I could barely swallow the Oreos still left in my mouth.

But I managed.

After a minute, I was still on my knees. I crawled back behind my desk and sat on the floor, sobbing, downing the last of the Oreos, and drinking milk from the carton. I leaned against the desk, not caring that the drawer handles poked into my back. Every minute or so, I stopped to blow my nose.

Josh was right this time, which made everything worse. It was one thing to be overweight. It was another to be found on the floor at work shoveling cookies into your face.

He'd never been able to fault my performance before. I'd always been perfect at my job.

I hiccupped a few times. I'd go back to being an impeccable performer. Then, let him try to work without me. He wouldn't last five minutes. He'd miss meetings, forget to return calls, offend all his clients. They would leave him in droves, saying, "I only stayed with you because of Bree." He'd be the one on his knees, begging me to come back.

In my misery, I clutched a piece of the empty Oreo bag and rolled over onto my side, finding a space for myself among the bits of cookie packaging. I lay there on the carpet.

Maybe I should just quit. I should tell him to take the job and shove it.

Maybe not. I shuddered at the thought of facing all those bills without a steady income.

"Bree?"

The voice startled me out of my dark thoughts.

"Where are you?"

As if I didn't have enough problems, now Lena was standing in the reception area. I lifted my head up off the floor, but she couldn't see me lying hidden behind my desk. I stared at myself in the giant mirrored wall, then lurched up to my hands and knees, my mascara dripping onto my blouse in giant black teardrops. "Down here," I said.

Slowly, her face came around the corner of the desk. She gave a little squeal at the sight of me.

I would never get used to how pretty she was, a dark brunette, her eyes a sparkling bright blue, framed by long lashes that curled. My eyes were a sun-faded version of the same color, with stiff, spiky eyelashes. Today she wore skinny jeans, a little sweater, and sandals, looking fresh and spectacular in her simple clothes.

"What are you doing?" she asked.

"What does it look like? I'm eating Oreos on the floor."

Lena's brow creased in confusion. "Why?"

"Why not?" Wearily, I stood up. "What's going on, Leen? Did you bring my shawl?" I knew she hadn't. She was here for her money.

"About my new place . . ." she began.

"Don't tell me you're moving again already!"

"No, nothing like that. But . . . it turns out I'm not rooming with Joanna." She paused, then added defiantly, "Stuart's moving in with me."

It took me a minute to remember that Stuart was just Boomer. "You're back with him now?" All those months of despair and weight gain, for nothing. Those two couldn't stick with anything, not even a breakup. "He's a cokehead!"

Her head went up, her shoulders back. "He's changed, Bree. He's in a twelve-step program now. It's helping him a lot."

Yeah, right.

"And I just joined the group for significant others of people with drug problems."

"Since when?"

"Since a couple of weeks ago. We're really serious about this."

Spare me. "That's great, Lena."

Her eyes dropped. "So, anyway . . ." She trailed off and fidgeted, looking at me expectantly.

No point in putting this off. I wrote out a check for a hundred dollars. "Don't cash this until tomorrow, okay?"

"Ah, living close to the edge, are we?" She swatted at me with the check, playful now that she had her payoff.

"Yeah, and whose fault is that?" I yelled, suddenly enraged. "After dragging me through the pits of despair for six months, now you're back together with that . . . that *addict*!"

She clenched her jaw. "He's getting help, which is more than I can say for you!"

"What're you talking about? I don't use any drugs!"

"Well, you eat enough to make up for that! Admit it, Bree. You're a food addict."

A food addict! "You got your money, which I'll never see again! Just leave, okay?"

Lena planted her feet. "You can't even admit it, can you?"

I was too busy for this. I had things to do. I had scripts to read, reservations to make, weight to lose. "You must have somewhere else to be."

"I do." She turned away, then back toward me. "Oh, and Bree? You got a little something right"—she put a finger on her cheek—"here!" She touched her chin. "And here." With a snarky grin, she strolled out the door.

I looked in the mirror. On my cheek and chin and forehead. Wet smears of chocolate cookie.

Fortunately, I didn't run into anyone on my way down the hall to the ladies' room. As my anxiety spiraled, I swished out my mouth and washed my face. It shone back at me in the mirror, pale and plump, like a sad moon.

Euthanize me. Give me a quick and merciful death. Without it, I would lose all control and hit the skids. I would sink, slowly, unconscious, deep into that great mass of the unwashed and the unpublished.

Five

I lay on my bed looking in the mirror and trying to see how much fat I could pinch between two fingers. I remembered that old thing about how if you could pinch an inch, you were overweight.

I could pinch three inches, at least.

As gloomy thoughts rolled through my head, an email came in. Kaitlyn again. I glanced at the time on my computer. Eight o'clock here in California, which meant eleven in New York. This woman was a machine.

> We've gotten you an interview on a video blog called Candace's Book Picks. She interviews authors and posts the videos online, and she's got 30,000 followers. She's based in LA, so you can interview with her in person—the sooner the better. Could you possibly squeeze it in on Monday at lunchtime? At her house in West Hollywood.
>
> P.S. Wear a vibrant color near your face—no white or black—and an interesting neckline, or maybe a scarf or necklace.

Not Monday. I would still be fat.

Why do I have to drive to her house? I wrote back. *Can't we use Zoom?*

She prefers face-to-face interviews. I could almost hear Kaitlyn growing steely again. *If you won't go, there are fifty other writers who will.*

I would go. What choice did I have? On Monday, Josh would have a lunch and some meetings, so I'd be able to sneak off and do it. I didn't want to buy new clothes for it, since I'd be losing weight over the next few months. What would I wear?

I already knew the answer.

The shawl was warm for LA in early May. I would look like a misplaced Greenlander next to all the girls in their little shorts and filmy dresses. But what else could I do?

Lena still had it, though, or I hoped she did. Given her casual approach to the care and maintenance of possessions, not to mention to the concept of ownership in general, she might have used it to mop up spills by now or donated it to a homeless person. Panicking, I punched Lena's code into my speed dial. She answered.

"Where's my shawl?" I demanded. "*Don't* tell me you don't have it!"

I paced the strip of carpet between my bed and the bathroom door, expecting a flippant non-answer, like, "What's the big deal? You never go anywhere anyway."

Instead, she said, "Can I give it to you Saturday? Stuart and I can drop by. Just for a minute."

Shocked but pleased, I asked, "Really? You would do that?"

"Sure."

"Which alien planet are you from, and what have you done with my sister?"

"I'm serious. We'll be there Saturday at five."

"Okay." This would be interesting.

It was 5:30, and Boomer and Lena were late. Taking into account her boyfriend's normal state of chemical impairment, I prayed Lena was doing the driving. It was a miracle he'd never had a DUI.

The hands on the clock crawled by. Worry for my sister, added to the existing fear about getting fired by Josh and losing my book deal, had me standing with my head in the refrigerator gobbling tater tots. They were cold and slimy eaten out of the fridge like that, but they served their purpose. I would feel better for about a minute until regret and indigestion set in.

It was 5:45. *She's fine, calm down.* It seemed like for all the times I wanted to murder Lena, I just as often feared losing her.

Six o'clock brought a knock at the door. I rushed to let them in.

"Hey, big sis!" Lena wore a white sundress and glowed with a contentment that turned her cheeks pink and put a sparkle of sapphire in her eyes. She clutched a shopping bag in one hand, and Boomer's arm in the other. "Here it is! I had it cleaned." She held out the bag.

Too astonished to speak, I took it from her. Then I looked at Boomer.

I had to hand it to Lena: she always got the hunkiest guys. Boomer was almost a parody of male beauty, with broad shoulders, classic features, and sun-streaked hair. Too bad I knew what was behind the façade: a coke-infused brain that focused mainly on surf conditions and board wax. That's why, though Lena called him Stuart, to me, he was clearly Boomer.

I hadn't seen him in over a month. His long hair, which usually straggled past his shoulders, was combed and neatly tied back in a ponytail. His eyes were clear. He wore a clean button-down oxford shirt tucked into jeans, a league removed from his usual tank top and board shorts. In the hand that wasn't holding Lena's was a huge blooming hydrangea plant.

Nicknamed "Boomer" at age twelve by his brothers because of his affinity for setting off explosives, he was heir to the Livingston textile fortune in South Carolina. He was the black sheep son who had gone to California to become a surfer. Lena had said he would come into a trust fund when he turned thirty, three years from now. But for the moment, he was on his own. Meaning he and Lena did odd jobs and mooched money off me and other spineless friends and family members.

"This is for you." He held the plant out. "In honor of your upcoming publication!"

"And here's a card." Lena pulled it from her purse.

As I slid the card from the envelope, two little pop-up frogs bounced out at me, bobbing up and down on springs. The printed portion of the card said, WE HOPE YOUR SUCCESS HAS YOU LEAPING WITH JOY.

"Thank you! Come sit for a minute." I poured myself a glass of wine.

"Just water," they said, speaking in unison.

"You guys didn't have to do all this." I gestured toward the bag, with my shawl neatly folded inside.

"*I* did," Lena said. "You've always had my back, no matter how much trouble I was in."

I wasn't used to appreciation from the girl I used to think of as "Mean Lena." We'd both always taken our roles for granted.

Lena was the one who got wasted at parties; I was the one who came to pick her up. I was the one who ran interference between her and Dad when she got caught smoking in the school bathroom or earned a D on her report card. Not that this was such a hard job, given he was tied up with work most of the time.

"Well . . . I guess you've got a point . . ."

"I'm done with that," she announced. "No more Little Miss Codependent!"

We'd see. I wouldn't easily forget her pregnancy at nineteen, which I'd helped her hide from Dad. Thankfully, he'd gone out of town on business, and the pregnancy had ended on its own soon thereafter.

"Are you guys going out to dinner?" I asked uncertainly. "You're so dressed up!"

"Yeah, actually, we're meeting my sponsor and his wife," Boomer said. "We're celebrating my first thirty days of abstinence. From drugs."

That's right. I remembered Lena said he'd joined a twelve-step program—some religious thing where God was supposed to solve your problems. Or something like that. I didn't believe in that stuff, but I was touched by the expression of love and pride on both their faces.

"Congratulations! Thirty days! I guess . . . that's pretty hard to do, isn't it?"

"It is," Boomer said, "but the group gives you lots of support." He dug in his pocket and produced a crumpled five-dollar bill, which he held out to me, catching me by surprise. "This is for you too, by the way."

"Why?"

"To start paying you back for the hundred you gave Leenie," he answered, surprising me even more. "It's not much, but there's more to come."

"So when you go to New York, will you be on an expense account?" Lena asked. "Will they let you, like, order room service and charge it to your publisher?"

"I think so." I'd actually been giving some thought to the mini-bar. But would the hotel itemize everything I ate on the room bill and send it to Fast Track? That would not do. "Anyway, I won't be in the room much. They say I'll be booked solid."

I wished I could look forward to it, but instead, the thought just made me tired. My stomach gurgled and pressed against my tight waistband. I wished I felt better, but all the recent sweets and fast food were coming back to bite me in my ample posterior.

"Aren't you excited?" she asked. "I mean, it'll be so glamorous going to fancy parties in New York. You'll be a celebrity!"

"Hardly." I found myself telling them about the terrifying marketing campaign and the red dress.

Having finished her own water, Lena reached for Stuart's glass. "Who cares if it doesn't fit anymore? Get something hot and sassy that fits you now." She sipped, then put the glass down.

"Are you kidding? They don't make great dresses in size 'blimp.'"

She patted her mouth with a napkin. "These days they have great dresses in any size. You could look fabulous—you just don't give yourself enough credit! Does she, Stuart?"

He rose to the occasion. "Nope! You're way hotter than you think, Bree."

They were naturally thin. They didn't know what they were talking about.

We stood to say our goodbyes. "You guys seem . . . good," I said as I hugged my sister. "You're, like, peaceful."

Her eyes filled as she glanced over at her boyfriend. "Yeah. It's because of Stuart. I think this twelve-step program is saving his life. And mine too."

"Because it got you off drugs?" I looked at him as I said it, including him in the conversation.

"Partly," he said, "but it's a lot more than that." Boomer pulled me in for a hug, my soft, puffy body colliding with an *oomph* into his hard chest and belly.

Oh, God, did he feel my fat? He was deliciously warm and smelled of saltwater and something else—maybe pine or eucalyptus. *Lena gets that every day—and more.*

Since Mark had left my life, I'd felt like a piece of driftwood on the beach—brittle, twisted, and deformed by the elements and the passage of time. Certainly not a girl a man would want to touch.

I squirmed away from Boomer. "Thank you," I said, raising the five-dollar bill. What would happen next? Maybe a beautiful man would arrive outside my window in a helicopter and sweep me off to Paris. It seemed just as likely as the behavior of these two right now.

"Okay," Lena said. "Love you."

"Same," I said.

I was still amazed an hour later.

Six

The day of my interview with Candace of Candace's Book Picks was way too hot for the shawl. I'd been badly and inappropriately dressed before, but with only a handful of people around and never in front of a camera. This time, though, my image would be immortalized on the internet and remain there until the end of time.

Not only would it exist forever, but it would be enlarged by the camera lens. Everyone knew the camera added ten pounds, not to mention the fact that Candace would probably shoot me at that unflattering three-quarters angle that you see in interviews, the one that catches your upper arm looking as wide as the state of Texas.

I was out of time and luck. I wore the shawl into the office, where by 10:00 A.M., sweat was trickling down the back of my neck. I survived the morning by myself, fielding frantic calls from Josh, who had managed to lose a crucial folder of notes I'd put in his briefcase.

After I'd emailed him the information he needed, I put up a sign saying OUT TO LUNCH—BACK IN THIRTY MINUTES and locked the office door.

It had seemed inadvisable to write BACK IN THREE HOURS. Josh would need me, clients would need me, but all office calls would go through to my cell, so I was covered.

Candace, the video blogger, lived in a yellow West Hollywood bungalow covered with bougainvillea vines and worked out of a converted free-standing garage in the back.

"Welcome!" She stood in her front doorway, distressingly slender in jeans, boots, a flowy blouse, and an assortment of bracelets and rings. Her eyes flicked over my thick black pants and voluminous fringed shawl, which I pulled at, trying to keep one side from drooping down to my ankles.

"May I take your . . . wrap?" she inquired, reaching for it.

"Oh, no!" I clutched it against my body. In addition to the usual areas to be covered, I had the new problem today that I'd had to leave my pants unbuttoned. Yet another thing to hide. "It's so chilly today," I said as I stepped into her living room, where sun poured through the windows, making pools of warm light on the hardwood floors. A gray cat stretched his body in the sunshine, yawning, then closing his mouth with a satisfied snap. I envied him. I wanted to be like him, luxuriating in the peace and quiet of my own home.

Funny how I was happiest when I was curled up on my sofa with my dearest friends, Fat and Sugar. Or when I was at my computer writing a story. By contrast, being interviewed on camera was like being skewered with a hot poker.

Candace studied me, her smile fixed in place. Only a growing tension in the corners of her eyes revealed any concerns that she might be hatching about this interview.

She wasted no time on small talk. "Follow me!" She led me out the back door and struck off through the yard and into her studio. A box of donuts sat on a wicker table. Two chairs standing before a white screen faced a video camera on a tripod.

She looked me over again. "Are you sure you don't want to take off that wrap?"

"My religion prohibits me from displaying my upper arms."

Candace laughed briefly but shot her eyes away from me, as if not sure whether I was joking or just very strange. "All right, let's get you settled." She put me in one of the chairs, clipped a microphone to my shawl, and set the camera running.

"I'm here with Sabrina Hunter, author of *The Passion of Cecily*, a historical romance featuring hotties and horses and coming in July," she told the camera. She turned toward me. "Sabrina, I loved your book so much. It's a roller coaster of a read!"

"Thank you, Candace!" It occurred to me that if my arm looked like the state of Texas from this angle, my shawl-covered body must look like the continent of North America. No wonder she had wanted me to take it off. Nonetheless, I plastered a smile on my face. "It's a pleasure to be here."

The interview was going to be torture.

"What is your normal writing routine?" Candace asked.

Climb into bed with my laptop and a bag of Skittles and write until I enter a sugar coma. "Gee, Candace, I just try to write for about four hours at the same time every day."

"What inspired you to write a romance?"

My need for hot imaginary sex. "I love a story with a happy ending!"

The questions dragged on. My hands shook and my head hurt from lack of nutrition. To make things worse, my cell phone interrupted us repeatedly with calls patched in from the office, forcing Candace to turn off the camera and wait. Frazzled, I whipped through each call, answering with a brisk "Josh Newman Talent" and firing instant answers back.

"Josh is waiting for the terms of the offer. He should have them today and will call you."

"You haven't received our package yet? I'll put a tracer on it."

"We've found a script that might interest you. I'll get it out to you this afternoon."

I hoped I sounded coherent. My brain was fogged over. Like a pilot without an instrument panel, it couldn't see where it was going. My stomach rolled sickeningly.

After sixteen light-years of agony, the interview finally ended. "Would you like a donut?" Candace offered. Ordinarily, I'd have refused. I never ate before witnesses, hoping to at least leave people open to the possibility that my weight stemmed from metabolic difficulties. "She never eats a thing!" they would say. Today, though, I was so rattled that I said yes, even though Candace was standing right there and my body was screaming for mercy. No sooner had I gobbled it down than I realized that I was in trouble.

"Excuse me, where's your ladies' room?"

"In the house."

I sprinted for it. I dashed into her little powder room just in time and, in a second, had tossed my cookies, something I never did. *That's it!* my body was saying to my brain. *No more! No more late-night taco runs. No more jumbo bags of Milky Ways in one sitting.*

I tossed the hot, sticky shawl into a corner and threw up again. Afterward, I remained squatting there for a few minutes, hunched over the toilet bowl, contemplating my glamorous first interview as a debut author.

The sound of boot heels on hardwood. Crap. Candace must be standing outside the door. Then I heard her voice. "Are you okay in there?"

Double crap. I had to answer. "I'm fine." I opened the door and stepped out.

Candace led me into the kitchen, where she wet a paper towel under the faucet and handed it to me.

"Thanks." I wiped my face, too embarrassed to look at her.

"You should rinse off your teeth," she said evenly. "Stomach acid ruins your enamel." Her expression wavering between recognition and sympathy, she added, "I've been where you are, believe me. Many times."

"You mean you . . . ?"

She shrugged. "Eat. Purge. I've done it for twenty years."

"It's not a way of life for me," I said. "I just eat and get fat. I mean, most of the time. Today, I think my stomach's upset." All of a sudden, I realized that the shawl lay in the bathroom while Candace viewed me in my sleeveless, unbuttoned splendor.

"You don't have to be fat," Candace ventured. "Not if you purge."

She had a point, but I couldn't imagine making myself throw up on purpose. "That's bad for you."

She shrugged. "Being fat is bad for you. If you're going to be unhealthy anyway, you might as well look good."

I'd never thought of it like that.

"Anyway, you're not that big. You don't need to walk around in a pup tent."

"Are you kidding?" I gestured downward to the area below my neck.

"Not at all. You're really pretty. You could put together some really nice looks if you made an effort."

Look nice now, while I was still fat? I tried to wrap my mind around the foreign concept. In my world, life started when you were thin. Being fat was like being in . . . whatever they called it . . . the pupa, or chrysalis, stage of life. You hung there, waiting on your little branch, and only if you got thin could you become a butterfly and live among the flowers.

"Come back out to the studio," Candace said. "I'll show you some of the footage."

We watched it in silence. Swathed in the brightly patterned shawl that glared against the white screen behind us, my body looked like a mountain rising through the mist, topped by a golf-ball-size head, and dwarfing the slender Candace sitting beside me.

The close-ups were even worse. I kept licking my lips while large beads of perspiration lined my brow. The sight was so ghastly I couldn't even listen to the interview.

Candace stopped it halfway through. "What do you think?"

"It's beyond horrible." I felt like I could talk to her, now knowing that she, too, was in the Sisterhood of Suffering. "I was going to lose weight before the book came out. And get some new clothes."

"Tell you what," she said. "You still have a couple of months, so go ahead. Lose weight, if you want, but definitely buy the clothes. In July, we'll reshoot the interview."

"Really? But Kaitlyn's expecting this one." I gestured to the image of a frozen me filling the screen, my mouth gaping open, my eyelids fluttering half-shut.

"I'll stage an accident," she said cheerfully. "And I can handle Kaitlyn. It'll be fine."

"Thank you." I left, not sure whether to regret that I still had to carry the burden of this secret or to feel relief that my secret was safe. For now, anyway.

I walked into Josh's office to find him already back from his meetings, looking for me and fuming. Not that I was behind on my work. Not that I'd missed even a single phone call. Josh was pissed off on principle.

"Where the hell have you been?" Sitting behind his desk, he seemed to swell in size like an inflating balloon. He was turning purple too.

"I had a personal errand to run. Everything's under control." In fact, I had totally bailed him out today when he lost all the notes I'd carefully prepared for him.

Josh opened his mouth to scream at me.

I was done. Done with this overgrown infant who couldn't take responsibility for his own life. As much as I hated myself, I hated him more.

Like a sleepwalker, I turned my back on him and went to my desk.

I needed chocolate relief. Listlessly, I pulled out a bag of Hershey's Miniatures from my drawer and poured a handful of the little candy bars onto my desk. Moving in slow motion, I picked up one in red paper and began to unwrap it.

Meanwhile, Josh had followed me into the reception area. "Don't walk away from me when I'm talking!"

"Sorry," I mumbled around a mouthful of candy. I'd never shown interest in so much as a peanut in Josh's presence, let alone the half dozen miniatures that I was robotically arranging into two parallel lines on my desktop. But it didn't matter anymore if he saw me. Let him fire me. Nothing mattered.

His eyes widened in disbelief. "Get that stuff off your desk now."

I gave him a cheeky grin. "I'm working on that!" With a flourish, my throat aching, I opened my mouth, popped in a Mr. Goodbar, and chewed. I looked down so I wouldn't cry, but I couldn't prevent the single tear that rolled down my cheek and plopped onto the dark surface of the desk.

I'd worked hard for this guy for three years. Why couldn't he act like a human being for once?

I didn't see Josh leave, but I heard him. Step by cautious step, he backed away, as if from a rabid animal, then disappeared, shutting his office door. He didn't deal well with true emotion.

Neither did I.

After a period of forlorn munching, I called Lena. "I can't take it anymore. I hate myself. I hate my life." Despite the closed door to Josh's office, I kept my voice low.

"What's wrong?"

Once again, I wondered who this stranger was, pretending to be my sister. The old Lena would have said, "You hate *your* life! Listen to this!" We would have talked about her for the next hour.

"I can't stand my job, and I'm not being straight with my publisher, and I *can't stop eating*." I wiped my nose with one hand and shoved a chocolate into my mouth with another.

"Hold on a second."

I waited, hearing Boomer's low voice in the background, then Lena's, and various rustlings. I squirmed. It seemed like Lena never did anything without him anymore.

Several more moments passed, where I heard more rustlings and the low tones of Lena and Boomer.

Her voice in my ear. "Bree? Will you promise to do something for me?"

"I dunno. What is it?" Something in her tone sent a tingle of suspicion through me.

"Just promise."

"No."

"Aw, c'mon, have I ever led you wrong?"

"Yes. Many times."

"Sabrina! Look . . ." She stopped for a minute, as if gathering her patience. "Stuart and I have been talking. He's been so happy since he joined this twelve-step program for drug addiction. And I told him about how you're addicted to food."

"I am not!" I said, wishing she would get off this obsession of hers.

"I'm trying to help you! They have meetings for compulsive overeaters, and there's one tonight."

"Forget it."

"Don't be such a butt! *Please,* Sabrina, just this one time!" Just for a second, she sounded like she was five years old again, and I was nine. After our mother had left us, I was trying to keep the world from breaking into pieces around us.

I could never turn my sister down. Not to mention the fact that she could be as easy to move as the Pyramids of Giza. I knew she'd never give in. "Where is it? And how long is it?"

"Promise you'll go?"

"Maybe. Well . . . okay. I promise."

Happy now, she turned bossy. "Get a pen and write down this address. Tonight at six thirty. Be there."

The All Saints' Church on Reed Street.

Trapped, with no way out. I would go, but I hadn't promised to stay for the whole thing.

Seven

The meeting room at the All Saints' Church was painted a sickly pea green. I perched on the hard seat of my folding chair, which I'd chosen for its prime location: in the back row by the exit. I'd be able to escape early for sure.

I pulled at my damp collar. If the green paint didn't drive you out, the heat would. Even with the windows open, my shirt stuck attractively to my back. Maybe that's how this program got you to lose weight, by sweating it off you.

At the front of the room, a row of chairs stood facing those in which the audience sat. I decided they had to be for the evening's presenters, allowing them to look at the attendees and speak directly to them. The bad part of this arrangement was that it also allowed speakers to spot any defectors sneaking toward the exit. This gave me pause until I decided I didn't care. They'd never see me again, nor I them.

A series of thumps resounded from the ceiling. "What's that?" I asked a girl on my right. She was really pretty, maybe twenty years old, with one of those perfect bodies that should have forever barred her entry to this room, as far as I was concerned.

She gave me a friendly smile. "The church rents out the upstairs room to a swing-dancing group. It helps them pay the bills, but it does make our meetings kind of . . ."

"Percussive?" I said, doubt growing in my mind.

"You could say that."

"Does the program rent this room for its meetings?"

She nodded. "We'll pass the basket later for rent money. They suggest three dollars, if you can afford it, but no one has to give if they don't want to."

I had to ask. "I hope you don't mind, but . . . you don't look like you've got an eating problem."

Her eyes widened. "Omigod, you should have met me two years ago. It's not that I was fat, although I truly believed I was." She paused. "I was *ruled* by food. My daily routine was: consume five thousand calories in a couple of hours, throw it all up, take laxatives, exercise for five hours and starve for ten, then start all over again. I would do anything to be thin. I popped amphetamines all day and had liposuction at age nineteen. That last thing was a birthday gift from my mom."

"Wow. I'm sorry to hear that." Here was yet another person whose normal weight concealed what could only be called aberrant eating behavior. It made me think of Candace, who threw up everything she swallowed.

Around us, the talk was beginning to die down and most of the seats had filled. "I'm Ariana," she continued. "Are you new? I've never seen you before."

"First time. I'm just checking it out," I said, thinking again of the back exit. Only five feet away, it promised fresh air and freedom. I still planned to give this meeting fifteen minutes, then bolt.

I discreetly checked my cell phone. A message from Kaitlyn. *We've set your launch date! July 17. Isn't it exciting?*

Wonderful. Further speech failed me, so I signed off with a couple of lame champagne glasses from the emoji selection.

Under different circumstances, it would have been exciting. Why did I have to go and gain all that weight? And why couldn't I lose it now? It was ruining what should have been the happiest time of my life.

That's why you're here. To lose the weight. Although now I only had nine weeks left. I wondered what kind of diet they followed.

The clock stood at 6:30. "Good evening." A presenter read from a page in a plastic sleeve. "My name is Nikki, and I'm a compulsive overeater and your leader for this meeting."

"Hi, Nikki," the group chorused back.

Upon Nikki's request, the group's treasurer reported, to scattered applause, a total of $37.12 in their checking account.

"Does anyone need a ride home?" Two hands went up, then more from people willing to help out.

"Our lead speaker for this evening will be Michelle," Nikki said, indicating a woman who sat next to her. The woman had a broad, plain face and unfortunate aqua-and-orange athletic wear, but there was something about her. She reminded me of warm cinnamon buns coming from the oven on a rainy day. Sweet and comforting.

To my eye, she carried ten to fifteen pounds of extra pudge. Smart of her to nip her problem in the bud when she still didn't have that much to lose.

"Hi, all!" Michelle waved to the group. "My name is Michelle, and I'm a compulsive overeater."

Voices rang back, "Hi, Michelle!"

"Will those who are also compulsive overeaters raise their hands?" Michelle asked. Hands shot up.

I didn't know what to do. Was I a compulsive overeater? I'd always had weight issues, but I'd never thought of myself in those terms.

At that moment, a guy slipped through the entrance door, raising his hand along with the others and taking an empty seat at the end of the presenter's row.

Michelle waved at him. He lifted his chin in acknowledgment and smiled back. A really adorable smile, which tempted me to inspect further. Shaggy hair, jeans, and dark blue sweater. A bona fide hottie.

His weight was normal. His age—I was pleased to see—was within boyfriend range.

An unfamiliar feeling stirred in me: interest.

Michelle resumed. "Please join me in the Serenity Prayer."

That settled it: I didn't belong here. God talk, group prayers— no thank you.

We bowed our heads, while all around me people recited the words together: "God, grant me the serenity to accept the things I cannot change, the courage to change the things I can, and the wisdom to know the difference."

"Do we have any newcomers here today?" Michelle read from the script.

I froze, trying to shrink myself out of sight, but next to me, Ariana was having a small fit, signaling and pointing at me. In desperation, I looked around me for other victims, but no hands had gone up.

Michelle caught my eye. "Hi. Would you like to tell us your name?"

I was apparently the only soul in the city of Los Angeles who'd gotten herself roped in as a newcomer to this meeting. "Um, hi, I'm Sabrina." I waved, trying to look friendly and relaxed.

Faces turned in my direction, smiling. "Hi, Sabrina! Welcome."

"Now I'll share for ten minutes," Michelle said. She paused for a moment. "I've been eating mindfully for two years on this program and have lost forty-eight pounds. I've also gotten a promotion, mended my relationship with my parents, and taken up sailing, which I'd dreamed of doing for years."

I wondered what she meant by "eating mindfully." I would have to ask someone afterward.

Michelle continued, speaking slowly, as if choosing her words carefully. "I've overeaten all my life," she said, her eyes misting over.

So had I.

Trying to push the thought away, I shifted my weight on the hard chair while my sweat trickled. The boots of swing dancers thumped above our heads.

"When my parents were fighting, I'd steal cookies from the kitchen, shut myself in my bedroom, and eat. I would buy or steal food and hide it in a Ziploc in the closet, in desk drawers, you name it. That way, it was always there for me when I needed it."

It reminded me of my food drawer at work. My eyes shifted over to the hot guy sitting a few chairs over from Michelle. How convenient that he was facing the audience so I could inspect him without being obvious. I tried to check his left hand for signs of matrimony but couldn't see anything.

"I came to the program ready to walk out if anyone tried to push God down my throat. Then, little by little, that changed. I began to see how faith in a higher power makes everything in my life better."

What color were his eyes? Hard to tell from this distance, particularly since he was looking sideways, toward Michelle. The green walls pressed in on me as I leaned forward, focusing on his even, white teeth and thick hair that waved just a little.

Michelle cleared her throat and paused again, thinking of what to say next. "I'd tried every diet and weight loss program in existence. But the worst thing was the voice in my head. The voice that said,

You're ugly. You're stupid. You never do anything right. Talk about bullying. The girl who owned that voice was the meanest bully around. And that girl was me."

Sudden pain burned in my throat and behind my eyes. Were there any more of those M&M's rolling around the bottom of my purse? But no, I couldn't eat M&M's in a meeting for overeaters.

Seeking distraction, I sneaked another look at Mr. Hottie. I needed to see that smile again. *Look at me.*

No luck. He was writing something on a large envelope that he carried with him.

"And yet, I would never have dreamed of talking to my two nieces that way. Or my sister or mother. I could speak with kindness and understanding to everyone but myself."

At that moment, Hot Guy looked up, his eyes meeting mine. He gave me a slight nod while I snapped my head in another direction, as if I hadn't just been caught inspecting every minute detail of his appearance, hoping he would look this way. My cheeks warmed. His eyes were a brilliant electric blue.

"Now I speak to myself in a loving, respectful manner. I'm happy at a size twelve. I could starve myself down to an eight, but I'd rather relax and eat a little more. And my husband thinks I'm sexy!" Michelle's plain face bloomed with happiness. "I'm so grateful for the people in this room. Thank you for your love and support."

She wiped her eyes as the audience applauded and gave whoops of approval.

Okay, so this person was the real thing. She had lived my life. *Big deal,* I told myself. *That doesn't mean you need this program.*

I couldn't ignore it, though. Michelle knew what she was doing. It was odd to think that those last fifteen pounds, which I'd assumed she was here to lose, weren't anywhere on her priority list.

Now what? Maybe they would talk about the meal plan. But no. Instead, Nikki asked, "Are there any birthdays?"

Were we ever going to talk about dieting?

My neighbor Ariana raised her hand. "Two years of mindful eating," she crowed.

Someone produced a candle, which we lit. After we sang "Happy Birthday," it was her turn to share. "I was never fat, but I didn't believe it. Two years ago, I thought I was going to die." She repeated the story she'd told me earlier.

"Now I eat three healthy meals a day, nutritious things like oatmeal, broiled salmon, and fruit. My life is sane. I'm so grateful for these rooms. Thank you."

"Congratulations!" I said in her ear, feeling happy for her success.

Now it was time for three-minute shares from anyone who wanted to talk.

"I'm Steve, and I'm a compulsive overeater. At my lowest point, I was drinking twelve to fifteen sodas a day and stealing my coworkers' food from the office refrigerator."

Omigod, I'd done that. I'd eaten Josh's meatball Subway sandwich, then had rushed to replace it before he noticed.

Another peek at His Hotness. Hallelujah—no wedding ring!

"I'm Jane. I was absolutely desperate when I came to the program. I couldn't stop eating. I came to lose weight, but what I cherish now is the peace of mind . . ."

With each new share, my chest constricted and my eyes stung. So many fears and feelings that resonated with me. I was relieved when the meeting came to an end, all of us standing in a circle holding hands and reciting the Serenity Prayer again.

As I started to leave, I felt a hand on my arm. It was Michelle, with my true love standing right beside her. My mouth went dry.

"Welcome!" she said. "Sabrina, this is Daniel." She nodded toward the guy I'd been ogling, who now had a name. Daniel. Danny.

Sabrina and Daniel. Bree and Danny.

"Hi, Sabrina," he said. He had a voice now too, a medium-pitched mellow voice seemingly created for the sole purpose of rolling through the syllables of my name.

He held out the bulky white envelope he'd been writing on earlier. "This is a welcome package," he said. "I've put my name and phone number on it . . ."

A faint hope arose that he'd fallen in love with me at first sight, but I forced myself to squash it.

"Since I'm the new member contact for this meeting, feel free to call me if you have questions. I don't want to impose by calling you."

"Oh, it's no imposition!"

His blue eyes went through me like lasers. "In that case, I'll call you in a day or two, then. Make a list of your questions." The exchange left me mute and quivering but still able to text him my phone number with a high level of speed and accuracy.

I said my goodbyes, slipped out immediately afterward, and raced to my car, thinking of my new acquaintance and future husband. It wasn't until I was halfway home that I suddenly realized I'd never asked about a food plan.

And I'd forgotten to leave early.

A day or two. That's what Daniel had said last night at the meeting. He would call me in a day or two.

I turned on my computer and pulled up my calendar for the week. Josh was holed up in his office with the door closed.

I was pretty sure Daniel really would call me. This was not a dating situation—in which case, all bets were off. No, he was the new member contact, and it was therefore his job to get in touch with me.

In a day or two, he'd said. Interpreting it literally, it meant sometime between this evening and tomorrow evening. As in . . . tomorrow.

Unless he didn't mean it as a specific promise, but more as a general estimate, in which case he might not call tomorrow, but within the next few days. Surely not longer than that.

The lack of certainty was maddening.

Line three was lit, meaning Josh was on the phone with Corinne. She had obviously kept her word and said nothing about the bracelet to her weasel of a husband. Or at least, I assumed as much, given the fact that I was still employed.

Nonetheless, when my cell phone vibrated, I answered it quietly, prepared to sign off right away if Josh emerged. We had still heard nothing from Alexa, which meant even more sour lemons from him than usual.

"Sabrina?"

I recognized the voice immediately. Omigod, he had called in less than a day! In fact, I did rapid calculations in my head. He'd called within twenty-one hours and three minutes! It had to be some sort of land-speed record.

"This is Daniel, from program."

"I know. I mean, hi!" Twenty-one hours and three minutes! That was way less than a day or two. What did it signify, that he was ahead of schedule? Welcoming the newbies was his job at the program, I reminded myself. He might just be a really good worker.

Or perhaps he was crazy about me, unable to stay away.

"So, do you have any questions for me since the meeting?"

Would you walk down to the beach with me? Talk to me and hold my hand? The light on line three went out. Eyeing Josh's door for signs of movement, I said, "Actually, I was wondering what your members do to lose weight. I mean, that's the point, right?"

"A lot of us do lose weight, yes. But the real goal is to get free of the obsession with food and eating. As we say, *it's the sanity, not the vanity.*"

"Did you lose weight?"

"Eighty pounds. It took me two years."

"Was it hard to do?" I tried to wrap my mind around the whole different person he'd been only two years ago.

"I had to learn how to eat mindfully—that is, how to pay attention to my body and only eat when I'm physically hungry."

I liked that part of it but still had my doubts. "But it's a religious program, right?"

"It's spiritual. We each define our higher power in our own way. Whatever makes sense to you."

I didn't think any way made sense to me. "Okay, I'll think about that."

"Just letting you know, some of us meet for dinner every week before program at the temple on California Street. You're welcome to come. Sam's Diner at five o'clock, and the meeting's at six thirty."

We'd both just been at a meeting the night before. I couldn't help asking him, "You're going to another meeting tonight?"

"I go to two or three meetings a week."

"Do most of you do that?"

"It varies, but yeah. A lot of us go that often."

Did these people do anything else with their time?

Josh's door flung open.

"I'll try— I'm sorry, gotta go!" I clicked off just in time.

Eight

Josh stood over me. "July seventeenth! It's our premiere date for *The Circus Murders*."

Shoot me and throw my body to the vultures. July seventeenth was also my book's publication date.

"We're doing something new, something really big: an after-party for three hundred people."

Impale me on a sharp stick and roast me.

"I've got other things on my plate right now. This'll be your baby—the entire event—location, concept, guest list, menu, logistics." Josh stopped to stare at me pointedly. "We really need a win right now, Sabrina. Don't screw it up."

When had I ever failed him? I resisted the urge to push him backward into his aquarium to lie there among the teeth-gnashing tropical fish. He wouldn't speak to me that way once I was a best-selling author.

Forget his party. I could plan it, but I wouldn't be there. This night in New York was my moment to shine. I wouldn't sacrifice it for a job I didn't care about.

But I did have a rather peculiar attachment to paying my rent. And galumphing down a staircase under a spotlight in a dress several sizes too small? Hard to see myself shining.

The Circus Murders might be my way out. If I pushed the amazingness of this Hollywood premiere, how important it was, how important *I* was for being associated with it, maybe I could get Fast Track to change the date of the *Passion* launch party and the theme to focus on something that was more . . . me.

Yet my throat ached at the thought of pissing them off and—who knew?—maybe losing my book deal.

As usual, Josh had an afternoon full of meetings. His last words to me as I bustled him out of the office were: "I'll need a creative concept for the party by tomorrow morning."

What did I want most, a career as a writer or a roof over my head? If I chose the roof, I'd need to do my best creative thinking today, and for that, I would need my mini chocolate peanut butter cups. I'd always found them to be inspirational, particularly those of the dark chocolate variety.

Then I had an idea. If I went with creativity—and the peanut butter cups—I could track the amount I ate, thus reinforcing my weight loss skills. Way to multitask!

My decision paid off. By the fourth peanut butter cup, I had envisioned a big top circus tent with groupings of tables and chairs mixed with open areas for dancing and mingling. Circulating through the crowd would be costumed circus performers: a stilt walker, jugglers, clowns doing magic tricks, performing animals, and an aerialist twirling overhead on a rope. In addition to really good food, there would be popcorn, cotton candy, and caramel apples.

My mind went into overdrive with all the things I had to do.

Call Kaitlyn and beg her to push my dates back a couple of days.

Find circus performers (that should be a breeze, ha ha, given the large number of jugglers and wild animal tamers in my contacts list).

Book a vacant lot and transform it with a floor and a circus tent.

Find a caterer who did circus-like food (*if* there was anything left in town on such short notice. And if there wasn't, find something fabulous anyway).

Go on a starvation diet, lose weight, and buy amazing clothes.

Or, if all else failed, make plans to trudge out into the wilderness and die.

Oh, and maybe I'd wedge in a couple of those twelve-step meetings. Not that they would do me any good, but I wouldn't mind another sighting of those brilliant blue eyes.

When Josh called (two peanut butter cups later), I pitched him my ideas, thinking they were really good. He said only, "Sounds okay—just make sure you're on top of it."

Make sure *I* was on top of it?

Someday, when I wrote a prize-winning international best seller and he wanted the movie rights, I would laugh in his face. *You should have appreciated me when you had the chance!*

But I still had to get my first book published, which meant I had to tell Kaitlyn my problem. Slowly, I typed a text into my phone. *Due to a prior professional obligation, I can't leave for New York before July 18.*

I stared at the screen, imagining Kaitlyn's eyes going stern and unforgiving. I couldn't believe I was about to piss off my brand-new editor this way. Yet another reason for Fast Track to cut back on marketing my book, or even drop me entirely. The thought was unbearable.

I amended the message to say: *Really, really sorry, Kaitlyn, but I'm responsible for the official after-party following the Hollywood premiere of* The Circus Murders, *starring Buck Billingsley. Therefore, I can't leave for New York before July 18.*

My thumb hovered over the send button as I wondered exactly how much Fast Track was going to hate me for this.

After a second, I highlighted the text and hit backspace. I would give it a day. Maybe a miracle would come along and save me.

It was all too much. My systems had gone on overload, their lights blinking the message, *Sabrina's brain is currently not available. Please try again later.*

I needed sleep and nutrition. I needed a clone of myself so I could be on two coasts at the same time. I gobbled my tenth peanut butter cup and wrote it down. It seemed like a lot, but they were the minis, after all, only about an inch in diameter.

I would do just a little more work, then meet Daniel and the others at Sam's Diner. I made a few calls and decided that, despite the wow factor involved, the party would not be improved by the presence of an elephant or large predatory cat. Elephants were unwieldy in cocktail settings, while lions were attack-prone and smelly. Neither of them was, well . . . potty-trained. I popped another peanut butter cup and decided we would have small performing dogs instead.

I produced a few miscellaneous snail mails, then got chocolate on them, thus reinforcing my preference for electronic communication.

Then Lena called with a dinner invitation for Wednesday and the good news that Boomer had found a wealthy client willing to pay big bucks for surfing lessons. "He wants one-on-one lessons for himself and each of his three sons! At fifty bucks a lesson!" she reported triumphantly. "We're in the money!"

"Awesome," I said. "See you Wednesday!"

It was four o'clock. My poor stomach gurgled, dutifully attempting to process the mountain of trans fats and simple sugars that I'd ingested over the last few hours. The giant mass would rumble its way through my intestines and inevitably settle in for a long stay on my ass and thighs.

If I'd had to eat peanut butter cups, I consoled myself, at least I'd tracked them. The final tally: a mere fourteen and a half of the little suckers.

Four thirty. My thoughts turned to Sam's Diner and Daniel. I hadn't expected to see Daniel today, or rather, to have him see me. Worse still, I didn't have time to go home and change.

Off to the ladies' room, where I inspected my teeth, swished out my mouth, and popped a Tic Tac. Hair—out of its scrunchie. Lena had always said men liked a woman's hair down, and she would know.

Plus, I had nice hair. I brushed and finger-fluffed it until it shone and rested softly on my shoulders.

Another Tic Tac for luck and a slow, sensual swipe of Kiss Me Quick lip gloss. Not amazing, but acceptable, I decided, smacking my lips at myself in the mirror.

The prospect of eating, however, made my insides churn.

On the drive to Sam's, I rehearsed a few clever gambits to pull out in the likely case that I felt dorky or insecure during dinner. I didn't need much, just a phrase or two to strike a jaunty note or maybe pave the way for a conversation about my glamorous Hollywood job.

I didn't feel very glamorous, though, standing outside the diner, taking deep breaths and gathering my courage. Shaky and light-headed, I adjusted my shirt to hide as much muffin top as possible. If necessary, I would clamp my large handbag over my belly and keep it there.

As I entered, I met an onslaught of shiny diner surfaces—glass, chrome, gleaming leather—and smooth girl-band music from the '60s. I found Daniel and Michelle with three other people organizing themselves to sit in a big booth near the back.

Daniel turned to greet me. "Sabrina! You made it!"

Flustered by his apparent pleasure at seeing me, I also couldn't help but notice that I'd been herded into the back of the booth to sit between him and Michelle. I didn't like booths on principle because they tended to jam you into a space with no belly room and no escape, but in this case, I was next to Daniel. I glanced over at him. Those eyes still captivated me, their color intensified by his navy flannel shirt, worn with the sleeves rolled up.

Michelle wore another athletic ensemble today, this one a sort of awful rust color with white stripes running down the sides. She beamed at me. "I'm glad you're here!" Her instant warmth made me feel at ease.

Seated in chairs across from us were three people in various stages of physical recovery, which I'd learned meant weight loss in program-speak.

"You guys, this is Sabrina," Daniel said to them.

I tried to remember their names, but I only picked up key details: a beard on the guy next to Daniel and a ruffled blouse on the woman beside Michelle. The woman at the far end of the table, opposite me, wore large hoop earrings.

"So how'd you like your first meeting?" Michelle asked me. She and Daniel turned toward me while the other three fell into their own conversation.

"It was interesting. I guess I'm still just taking it all in."

"Michelle and I started the program on the same day," Daniel said. "Three years ago." He lounged, completely at ease in the crowded booth, while I squeezed my arms tightly against my ribs, trying not to brush up against him. It seemed too . . . personal.

"So he started hanging out with me and James. My husband," Michelle said.

"And after I'd lost about fifty pounds, James got me involved with his hiking group."

"And then, after Daniel got to be a hottie, I became his body-guard!" Michelle said.

"That bad, huh?" This was turning out to be more interesting than I'd expected.

Daniel shook his head. "Don't listen to her."

"His regular meetings have skyrocketed in female attendance," Michelle told me. "It's a known fact."

"Sabrina," Daniel cut in, giving Michelle a pointed look, "what do you do?"

I almost said, "I just sold a book," but a thread of superstitious fear stopped me. I still half believed that Fast Track would change its mind when it learned I'd, um, *outgrown* the red dress. Or what if I jinxed the deal just by talking about it?

"I work for a talent agent." I told them about my job and the *Circus Murders* party. Michelle peppered me with questions while Daniel listened, sitting with one bare forearm and hand resting on the table. My eyes lingered over his tanned wrist and fingers, pictur-ing them circling around my own wrist and hand.

My cell phone detonated, signaling a call from Josh. Although it was after office hours, that wouldn't stop him if he were really agi-tated about something. "Speak of the devil," I said, hastily pushing a button on my phone.

Josh had one of those voices that carried. It blared out into the space around us.

"I need those courtside Lakers tickets now! Where are they?" Josh was favoring a few lucky people with hard-to-get tickets to the NBA finals.

Hemmed in on either side, I could not escape to a private corner. "I told you about this, remember? They're being messengered. We'll have them first thing tomorrow morning." The final game was tomorrow night, which was closer than I myself would have cut it, but Josh specialized in last-minute crises, the sorts of things that permanently aged you. Fortunately, I had a ticket broker who could perform miracles not seen since the days of Moses. If Felicia said I would have the tickets on time, I would have the tickets on time.

Josh's voice rose half an octave. "You should have been on top of this!"

"But—"

Daniel appeared to concentrate on his tea bag, dipping it in and out of the water, while Michelle toyed with her fork.

Josh's voice continued to boom out of my phone, filling the space around us. "Don't argue with me. Go get them and bring them to me. Now."

"It's dinnertime! They're closing."

"I don't care. Skip dinner if you have to. Just get those tickets."

Daniel snorted at that one, while Michelle sucked in her breath. Livid, I dug my heels in. "This is completely unnecessary. We'll have the tickets by ten tomorrow morning, guaranteed. The game's not until eight P.M."

The information slowed down Josh's juggernaut of urgency. "Guaranteed?"

I glanced at Daniel, who'd stopped stirring his tea. Across from him, Michelle sat quietly. They were both openly listening now.

"I'm hanging up, Josh."

"Well, okay." Josh was downshifting from enraged to sulky. "I guess we can wait," he added, his tone indicating just how big a concession he was making.

"Right." I clicked off and looked up to see Daniel roll his eyes.

"That was your boss?"

"Yeah. He's . . . awful."

"We figured that out," Michelle said, her gentle tone comforting me.

The waiter arrived, only to be told we needed a minute. My insides twisting and turning, I tried to think about ordering. Hoop Earrings at the other end advised me to stay away from the borscht, but that the other soups were good, while Ruffled Blouse suggested I get the salad dressing on the side, because the kitchen poured with a heavy hand.

I couldn't even open my menu. After days of bingeing, topped with today's parade of peanut butter cups, my system was in full revolt. My gut surged over the waistband of my pants, while inside my stomach bucked like a bronco. "Just some more tea, please," I murmured to the server.

No one questioned my decision not to eat, nor had there been any talk of dieting, calories, or portion control. Daniel ordered a turkey sandwich with coleslaw, and Michelle a large salad. The others ordered salads with soups or sandwiches.

"How long have you been in that job?" Michelle said. "If you don't mind my asking."

"Three years."

They nodded, their eyes full of sympathy.

My face burned again.

The bearded guy next to Daniel piped up. "Your higher power will guide you if you let him."

Binge

Daniel cut him off in a flat voice. "Your boss is a dick. You shouldn't have to put up with that."

Michelle gave a startled laugh. "No point in holding back, Daniel. Tell her what you really think."

Hearing Daniel leap to my defense, I felt a warm spot begin to grow in my chest. I was about to say, "It's okay," but I stopped myself. It wasn't okay. His eyes bored into me, angry, and maybe a little embarrassed by the strength of his reaction. Scattered within the brilliant blue of those eyes, I realized suddenly were flecks of green.

"I can handle Josh," I told Daniel, as the warm spot spread inside me. "I'm just biding my time. Thanks, though." I dipped my tea bag into my cup.

"Do you have a sponsor?" he asked me.

"No, do I need one?"

"Eventually," Daniel said. "But take your time. Sponsors need to be compatible with their sponsees."

"*Sponsees?*" I laughed at him. "Is that a word?"

Daniel's eyes widened in surprise. "I never thought about it. Probably not normally," he admitted. "But in twelve-step meetings, yes, it is a word."

"How do I find out who the sponsors are?"

"I'm a sponsor," Michelle said. "But there are a lot of us. Come to a few meetings and look around until you find one whose style matches yours."

"Thanks—I've got a lot to think about."

During the last moments of dinner, I learned that Michelle ran a daycare center and her husband was a sound engineer. The two of them had moved here four years ago from Texas so James could find work in the film industry. To my disappointment, the talk didn't extend to Daniel's background.

It was time for our meeting, so we headed off for our cars. I wanted to go home, but as my car was caravanning between Michelle's and Daniel's, I couldn't find a way to sneak off unnoticed. So I went to the meeting and stared at Daniel's profile and finally fell into bed at ten o'clock, my head spinning with thoughts of mean bosses, blue eyes, and big top tents.

Nine

Lena and I drank sparkling cider on her giant purple thrift-store sectional sofa while Boomer stirred things and banged pots in the kitchen. He was making beef stew for our Wednesday night dinner, a fearsome prospect. I tried to keep an open mind. "If it doesn't work out," he had promised me, "we've got Saltines and peanut butter."

He emerged in a minute with another bottle of cider in his hand and Lena's annoying little dog under his arm. Of mixed heritage, Twinkie was an ill-tempered creature with a pushed-in face and grotesquely bulging eyes.

"Stuart, show Bree what he can do," Lena commanded.

What was she talking about? The Twinkie I knew didn't do anything more than snarl at your ankles.

Boomer placed Twinkie on the empty coffee table and motioned with his hand. "Dance!"

After a moment of encouragement, Twinkie was up on hind legs and prancing across the table.

"Whoops!" Lena caught him as his jump carried him off the edge of the glass. "Better get you down a story." She placed the dog on the rug.

I watched her, smiling at the change in her over the last few months. That sharp little line of discontent that used to sit between her eyebrows had completely vanished. Her lips curved upward, and her cheeks glowed pink.

"Sit! Down! Roll over!" Boomer focused intently on Twinkie as the little dog went through his paces.

Then, "*Bang, bang!*" Boomer made a gun with his fingers and pointed at Twinkie, who collapsed in a heap, his legs sticking comically up in the air. Lena and I clapped while she explained, "Stuart trained Twinkie to do all this stuff!"

"I'm impressed, Boomer." Lena's boyfriend apparently had skills that emerged when he wasn't coked up.

Boomer went to check his stew while Lena and I talked. As Lena sipped from her glass, her eyes avoided mine. "I tried to call Dad today."

Our dad, the ultimate absentee father. I put down my drink, hearing the sharp *clink* of glass hitting glass. "What for? Are you kidding?"

I knew I shouldn't have come to dinner. I should have stayed at the office, proofreading the party invitation and finishing the guest list. But Lena and Boomer had insisted, and now this. Lena had gone over to the enemy. My breathing quickened.

"When are you ever gonna forgive him, Bree?"

I leaned toward her, as if somehow that would persuade her. "You were too little to remember what he put us through. What he put *me* through. I protected you from all of that!"

When I was twelve and she was eight, I made sure she got breakfast and had clothes to wear to school. When I was twenty, attending Dartmouth, I tried to enforce rules for her over the phone about homework and curfews, trying to make her life in LA as normal as possible. Meanwhile, Dad, who lived in the same house with her but was gone fifteen hours a day, stayed emotionally on his own distant planet, barely aware she was alive.

Pain began to form again in lines around Lena's eyes. "I think, if we asked him about those times he left us on our own, he'd say he was sorry."

"Too little, too late!" I snapped.

"Anyway, I couldn't reach him. His number's disconnected." Lena's downturned mouth showed her disappointment.

"What did he do? Move again without telling us?"

Lena's face wrinkled in distress. "I don't know what he did. I hope he's okay."

I exploded. "Omigod! He doesn't give a shit about us." A flash of pain surprised me. I'd thought I was long past being hurt by my father.

Pushing it out of my mind just didn't work. I'd tried for years. The truth was, I didn't want to forget what my father had done. And I most certainly didn't want to forgive him.

"Dinner's ready in five minutes!" Boomer called from the kitchen. Now living together, he and Lena had merged their belongings in a way that was uniquely them. Four surfboards leaned against the dining room wall, side by side, their patterns of brilliant reds, blues, and greens enlivening the room like some kind of accidental real-world work of art. "Stuart had them in the closet, but I took them out," Lena had told me. "I mean, they were begging to be seen!"

Their coffee table featured the abandoned Mercedes wheel that Lena had spotted beside the freeway and collected after screaming at me to pull over. She'd removed the tire and placed a circle of glass on top of the metal wheel. Her chairs were former junkyard residents that she had rescued and reupholstered herself. She'd done the bathroom herself too, wallpapering it in old four-color comic book pages, shellacked into place.

Lena lit candles, which warmed the room, and we ate sitting on the floor around the wheel table. When Lena wasn't looking, Boomer fed bits of the beef stew to Twinkie; the stew was meaty with a pleasant kick. "It's good!" I mumbled with a full mouth, nodding toward the stew pot. I took another slab of baguette. It made me feel guilty, but I couldn't be rude to Boomer after he'd gone to all this trouble. As embarrassing as it was, I was still writing down everything I ate. I mentally added *one-half French baguette* to my list for today.

Leaning against the sofa, Boomer wrapped a lazy arm around my sister's shoulders, while Twinkie wiggled himself in between them. "So, Leen," he drawled in his Dixie accent. "Should we tell Bree why we invited her here tonight?" He kissed the top of her head.

Omigod, Lena's pregnant. It was my first thought. They were going to have some awful shotgun wedding that would destroy my sister's life, wiping out any chance she had to go back and finish college or get a really decent job. She'd be waiting tables to support her derelict husband, or worse, I'd be supporting them both. I gripped my glass of cider, feeling faint.

Lena made a show of clearing her throat. "Yes," she said, "we have invited you here . . . to make amends!"

"You . . . what?"

"Amends," Boomer said. "It's one of the twelve steps. You make amends to the people you've hurt." He glanced over at Lena. "Should I start?" He pulled a piece of paper from his pocket.

"Are you still growing that Superweed?" I wondered if he had put it in the stew.

"Of course not." He frowned at me. "I'm clean and sober now." He began to read from the page.

"Sabrina Hunter, I'm sorry for all the times I was stoned in your presence, and all the times I gave grief to your sister, and therefore to you." His beautiful face was solemn underneath his hair, pulled up in a topknot and secured with one of Lena's puffy scrunchies. "Specifically, I'm sorry, first of all, for setting your wicker wastebasket on fire." He paused. "With that joint I thought had gone out," he clarified.

"Second, for hiding my stash in the trunk of your car without telling you." He shot me a cautious look as I processed that interesting new tidbit.

"Three, for eating all your brownie mix and freezer cookie dough while stoned. Four, driving Leenie around while high and making you worry. Five, borrowing money and not repaying it."

He dug again in his pocket, producing a couple of bills. "Twenty-five more dollars," he proclaimed, handing them to me. "I'll have the rest of it paid in a month. Oh, and I have this too." He left the room and returned with a wastebasket similar to the one he'd incinerated. Inside were two boxes of brownie mix and two rolls of frozen cookie dough. "For you."

I gasped. "Cookie dough!" With a knife from the table, I cut off the plastic at the end and peeled it back, then offered a wedge of the frozen dough to each of them. *It's chocolate chip, the equivalent of heaven,* I thought, as I inhaled a chunk.

"My turn to make amends now," Lena said. She had taken two nibbles of her dough, then handed the rest to Boomer, while I cut myself another thick slice and munched through it.

Then I realized what I'd done. Faced with a lethal trigger food, I had once again forgotten about how I had to get thin for my job and my trip to New York, forgotten about everything—in fact, gone into an eating trance, and only emerged now, eight hundred calories later.

"Excuse me! I'm talking here." Lena glowered at me from beneath her bangs. "You gonna listen to my amends or not?"

"Oh, yeah, sorry." I pulled my attention back to their living room.

"All right then," she said. "I can't pay you back what I owe, at least not right away, but I can make some other promises. First off, I will pay my own way from now on. No more coming to you for money."

I didn't see how she planned to keep that promise, as Lena and employment had not historically coexisted well together. Maybe she thought Boomer would help her.

She took a deep breath. "I will never again move in with you for long periods of time. I will listen to you about your problems, like you do about mine. I will take care of you, as you have taken care of me." Lena began to leak tears. "You're my big sister, and I love you."

"Aw, honey." I crawled over to her on my hands and knees, Boomer obligingly moving back so I could throw my arms around her. "I love you too."

We hugged and sniffled for a few minutes until I moaned, "I can't believe I have to leave soon and go back to work."

"Tonight? What for?" Lena's eyes widened in bafflement.

"I've gotta work on the party. I'm desperate to find a caterer. And I've got to review book jacket copy and press releases for Kaitlyn." Fear twisted inside me. I still hadn't told Kaitlyn, who had booked me for three events in New York on the seventeenth, the day of the party. What an idiot I was. By not telling her about my scheduling conflict, I'd made a bad situation ten times worse.

Lena brightened. "I know a great caterer. Olivia Landers. When I was temping, I worked a bunch of events for her, remember?"

I'd heard of Olivia Landers. I made a mental note to call her. "Weren't you a file clerk when you temped?"

"Sometimes. But the better temp jobs were with Olivia. I set up trays and passed appetizers to guests—it was a big responsibility." Pride infused her voice.

"Sounds like it." Another wave of fondness for my little sister brought tears to my eyes.

I didn't usually tell her my problems—my role was to solve *her* problems—but I found myself blurting out some of the random thoughts that had been brewing in the back of my mind.

"I'm terrified the launch party'll fizzle, and I'll never get another publishing deal."

Lena and Boomer were glued back together by this time. They sat quietly on the floor, cross-legged, holding hands and listening, while Twinkie rested his chin on Lena's knee. "Honey . . ."

"I don't know what to do, Leen."

"You're doing your best."

Boomer spoke up. "No, she's not."

"Stuart!" Lena drew in a sharp breath and pursed her lips.

"I'm serious. This editor lady's trying to work with you, Bree, and you're just dinking around with her, leaving her in the dark about this big problem. She needs to know!" Boomer's face was so earnest and troubled that it was hard for me to take offense.

"I don't want to disappoint her." I explained about my plan to lose the weight. "The problem is, instead of losing, I've actually gained five pounds . . . you know, from stress eating . . . and now with only eight weeks left, I've got to lose over five pounds a week to make it happen. But I can do it!" I nodded at them. "And I'll work out the date conflicts . . . somehow. It'll all happen."

It sounded good as I said it, but a knifelike pain entered my skull while Lena and Boomer exchanged glances.

We sat in silence for a moment until Lena jumped up. "Let me get you Olivia's card."

Twinkie at her heels, she vanished behind a row of hanging strings of beads that clicked against each other as she passed. I wouldn't have been surprised if Boomer had followed them like a second adoring puppy. It would have driven me crazy, but she seemed to like their intense togetherness.

"Hey, Bree," Boomer said. "Can I ask you a favor?" He lounged on the floor as if on a fashion billboard, his arm on the seat of the sofa, his long legs stretched out, and his head thrown back.

Uh-oh. He probably wanted his twenty-five dollars back. "Yes."

"Would you call me Stuart from now on? I kinda want to leave the Boomer days behind."

"Oh! Sure. I didn't know you minded that name." I felt my cheeks turn red. Had I been insensitive?

His eyes dropped almost shyly. "I didn't, until recently."

Lena returned, brandishing a lavender business card. Boomer—Stuart—greeted her like she was just back from a long Antarctic expedition, nuzzling her neck and openly French-kissing her.

I used to think Stuart and Lena's gropings were kind of *yeesh*, but today they seemed sweet. I hadn't thought about kissing a guy in a long time, because after all, that was for thin girls who didn't mind being touched.

Ten

At noon on Friday, I slipped into the seat of another uncomfortable metal folding chair. I couldn't believe I was taking a lunch hour to go to program when things were so busy, but Josh could hardly claim I wasn't working enough. I'd been up until two in the morning preparing a party budget for him to review. My throat felt scratchy, and my neck and shoulders ached.

Yawning, I peered around the dreary meeting room. Of course, I wasn't looking for anyone in particular. I was there purely for spiritual recovery.

That's why I couldn't have cared less when Daniel walked in, surrounded by women. Michelle had been right. The female-to-male ratio around Daniel far exceeded that of the room overall.

From what I'd seen of him in meetings, he was nice to all the girls and women in his orbit—not just the recovered, but also the flailing, the sagging, and the sad. Of course, that's why he was nice to me. Who was I kidding? He liked me in exactly the same way that he liked kind, obese seventy-year-old Bertha B., who snorted when she laughed.

He had cut his hair. No longer shaggy, it revealed a profile and jawline so unexpectedly appealing that my internal organs dropped a yard or two. This was just not playing fair, as far as I was concerned. He caught sight of me from across the room and waved.

I waved back, causing my bag to slide from my lap and spew its contents, including things of high caloric content that I preferred to keep private. By the time I'd scooped them all up, Daniel was seated and we were beginning. I had learned that a different member gave the lead share at every meeting. Today it would be Haley G.

My abused stomach grumbled, this time from the not entirely unpleasant feeling of physical hunger. I had managed to eat a normal-size bowl of oatmeal with blueberries and bananas earlier for breakfast. Like a plant that's been watered after a long drought, my body was already perking up, reviving with the help of this unexpected blast of nutrients.

It was refreshing to feel my body actually physically hungry for more nutrition instead of what usually drove me: my mind craving empty calories to avoid all the thoughts and memories I couldn't handle.

My cell phone vibrated to indicate a text was coming in. It was Kaitlyn. *I'm so excited! I've emailed your preliminary schedule for the launch promotion. Plan to arrive on July 16, as we start bright and early the next morning. You return home on the 18th. Here's to a spectacular launch!*

Run me over right now. Leave me for roadkill. Boomer—or rather, Stuart—had been right. Due to sheer wimpy indecisiveness, I had let this thing spiral out of control. Why hadn't I told her immediately? She could have possibly delayed the launch, or postponed a few early events, but now there was no chance. I was totally, irretrievably screwed.

Hayley G. was talking to us. "I'd been labeled fat my whole life. I was so angry and defiant—it was like I hated the whole world, myself most of all." Her voice trembled.

Angry. Defiant. Out of control. Didn't sound a thing like me. My throat was getting scratchy, so I cleared it a couple of times.

The room was silent as we all waited for Haley's next words. She took a deep breath. "My sponsor and I talked about the ways I'd always eaten to mask bad feelings, like my anger from the past that kept me from connecting with people. But I'm getting to know people and making friends! And I'm so grateful for that."

She sat down to a storm of applause while I clapped along, thinking, *It would be nice . . .*

If it were true.

Did things really work that way? I wasn't sure I could believe it.

Announcements were made, and people began to share. My cell phone continued to vibrate as several more texts and voicemails came in; yet another was from Kaitlyn.

On Monday I'll be sending you a few last notes where I think the story would benefit from some more interior monologue from Cecily, some place description, etc. Your prompt response would be appreciated. Thanks!

I would keep my evenings open next week so I could jump on the work when it came in. If I couldn't cut it in the glamor and glitz department, I would make up for it by being perfect in all other ways.

I let my mind go back to wandering. I imagined myself thin, wearing skinny jeans and a tight sweater, with one of those big fashion scarves wrapped around my neck. I was sitting with Daniel on a deck sipping white wine. I whipped off a witty remark, causing him to laugh ruefully, then take my hand in a sudden rush of emotion. "From the first moment I saw you," he said, bringing my hand to his lips—

"Sabrina?"

I looked up mid-fantasy to find the real thing standing in front of me. The meeting was over. People were heading out the door or milling about and chatting as they got ready to leave.

"Glad you could make it for another meeting," he said.

Daniel seemed to be pretty much a jeans guy, with a variety of shirts, always with the sleeves rolled or pushed up. Today it was a basic white cotton button-down, the jeans a well-faded blue. To me, it was male fashion at its finest.

When Daniel smiled, his cheeks creased, his eyes got all warm and intimate, and he looked directly into you, as if he thought you were really, really special. No wonder all the women came flocking.

He was smiling now. "How's it going?"

"It's going well!" I searched for something to say. "Uh, I had oatmeal this morning."

He nodded, eyes twinkling. "Good choice." He held out a flyer. "Softball game at the park down the street from here. It's next week, by open invitation of the Wednesday night Conscious Eating Group."

I didn't have time for this. I accepted the flyer anyway. I heard myself saying, "Can I just spectate?"

He took on a light teasing tone. "Only if that's really a word."

"Oh, I assure you it is." Braver now, I ventured, "Are you playing?"

"You bet. C'mon. You sure you don't wanna play? We can always use people."

I bit my lip. I had to admit, it sounded fun. In middle and high school, I'd played some softball, and I'd been okay at the batter's plate, usually able to get off a hit.

It was Friday. I'd be working on the *Circus Murders* party over the weekend and making Kaitlyn's changes on Monday and Tuesday evening. Why not take a little break next Wednesday? Who needed sleep, anyway?

"I'll drop by, but no promises about playing." Even as I said it, I knew I wanted to.

"Great," he said. "I'll see you then."

As I watched him go, I fumbled for my cell phone and retrieved my messages: the caterer, Olivia Landers, inviting me and a guest to a sample tasting reception; the acrobatic troupe canceling due to a scheduling conflict; and Josh ranting about the cost estimate I'd given him.

My mind sorted through them. The tasting reception would confirm Olivia as caterer for the *Circus Murders* party and help create the menu; I RSVP'd yes. I would also have to replace the acrobats, but with who? I couldn't book the magician I'd seen—in that one trick, it was obvious he'd had the rabbit hidden under his coat. As for Josh, I would go over the budget one more time to be sure I was doing this party for the lowest cost possible. After that, he would just have to trust me.

At the office, I ignored my work, brooding. I hadn't lost any weight yet, even though I'd written down every particle of cookie dough and French baguette I'd eaten, not to mention those nachos. I had so far gotten away with my secret fatness through the kindness of Candace's heart, but a showdown with Fast Track was approaching.

Seated at my computer, I entered the following words into a search box: *recipes for thirty-day juice fast.* I took a pen and started an ingredient list.

Kale. My pen made deep scores in the paper.

Oranges. Fresh mango. I'd learned that the program left our eating plans up to us, so theoretically I could follow this one, right? There wasn't anything wrong with it, was there?

Good thing I didn't have a sponsor yet. The fast was temporary, anyway.

I finished my shopping list, then stared at Josh's closed door. I couldn't do any more work on the party until I cleared the budget with him.

I knocked on the door and popped my head in. "Excuse me. Do you have time to discuss those cost numbers?"

He looked up from his glass-topped desk, startled. His normally pinkish complexion began to darken. "Just cut them by twenty-five percent."

"A twenty-five percent cut means no aerialist, no performing dogs, and no shrimp on the buffet."

Josh made a strangling noise. "That's ridiculous! Find cheaper performers."

"Can't. Not if you want performers who are liability insured."

Josh glowered at me, his face now verging toward an eggplant color.

"I think I can cut ten percent, though, without giving up anything important. Do you want to hear how?" I was proud of myself for having found a handful of corners where we could cut costs painlessly.

He was already turning his attention to his cell phone. "No. Just do it. And shut my door on your way out."

I let the door slam behind me. The minute I got my advance, I was out of this place. Fuming, I just happened to brew Josh's afternoon coffee at double strength, knowing it would keep him up all night. I would definitely go to that softball game on Wednesday, even if it meant ducking out at five to go home and change first. If Josh didn't like it, that was his problem. I had a life to live.

Eleven

You're not going to stay long, I told myself as I approached the softball field. Kaitlyn's editorial comments had come to me yesterday, and they needed my time and attention. I would play softball for an hour, then leave; I had a late night of work ahead of me.

The field we were using occupied a corner of a city park and was nicely appointed with bases and enclosed by a chain-link fence. Grass covered the field except in the paths that ran between the bases, which were bare dirt. I'd cleverly chosen to wear an outfit that didn't look as if I came intending to play but would allow me to play if I wanted. It consisted of jeans, sneakers, and a long, dark tunic that camouflaged the areas of my body that needed it most.

As I walked up, teams were forming. Daniel motioned me over. "This is Bree," he announced to the group around him. Somehow, he had transitioned into using my nickname, which only family and close friends ever used. Hearing him say it gave me a warm glow.

"Hi." I gave a little wave, relieved to see a number of bodies that were still on the way to full physical recovery. My chubby self had company.

This gathering had a disproportionate number of men, by program standards; about a third of the group was male. We needed every person there to make up two full softball teams.

"Any particular skills?" Daniel asked me. "Can you hit the ball? Throw it?"

"I can catch." I'd always been good at the egg toss at the neighborhood Fourth of July barbecue. Within moments, I found myself squatting behind home plate while a batter two feet in front of me awaited the first pitch.

From Daniel.

We all laughed as he made exaggerated—and meaningless—hand signals to me, wound up elaborately for the pitch, then eased the ball gently over the plate. The batter swung and missed. I caught the ball and waved it happily around until someone pointed out I should return it to Daniel. My throw made it about two-thirds of the way, then bounced toward him while he scrambled for it. The rest of our team whooped and hollered. "Strike one!" someone called.

We were off to a promising start.

"That was fun!" I said to Daniel later. The game's score was undetermined, as we had forgotten to appoint a scorekeeper. Both teams claimed victory. I was just glad that I'd caught more balls than I'd dropped. I'd hoped to get a hit but had managed only two walks instead. At least I hadn't disgraced myself by striking out.

People were taking off for home and family; it was a Wednesday evening, after all. I'd retrieved my bag and was saying my goodbyes when Daniel came up to me with Michelle, who'd ridden to the game with him, and another woman, Jackie. "Do you want to catch a bite with us?" Daniel asked me. "There's a Thai place on the next block."

I had a good three to four hours of work to do on *Passion*. I would have to say no. "Sure, I'll go!"

Say no to dinner with Daniel? Not gonna happen. At the same time, I had no intention of letting Kaitlyn down. I would get her work done. I would pull an all-nighter if I had to.

The four of us set off down the street, but as we reached the restaurant, Jackie got a call. She grimaced, her eyebrows knitting together. "The baby's got a hundred-and-three-degree fever. I have to go."

Michelle suddenly sprang to life. "You know, I think I'll catch a ride with you, Jackie, and have dinner with my husband. You don't mind, do you? I'm right on your way." She beamed at me and Daniel. "Sorry, guys. You might as well stay and enjoy dinner." She hustled Jackie off in the direction of her car.

Could she have been any more obvious? All of a sudden, Daniel and I were going to dinner by ourselves. Just the two of us. Like on a date.

We stood there, looking at their retreating backs and not at each other, until Daniel opened the door to the restaurant.

I felt my face go warm. He couldn't possibly want to do this. "We can go another time," I started to say, but Daniel simply said, "After you." He gestured to the doorway, which I swept through as nonchalantly as I could, my heart knocking against my ribs.

Once seated, I scoped him out, looking for signs of restlessness or longing glances toward the exit. He calmly studied the menu. "They have good curry here," he said, looking up.

Our eyes met. I was glad I was sitting down so my knees couldn't buckle.

"Where do you work?" I asked.

"A place called the Foundation for Justice. I'm a lawyer."

Another lawyer, like my ex. "What kind of law?"

"Immigration. We help people seeking citizenship or residency in the US." The enthusiasm in his voice energized me. "It's an exciting area these days."

He picked up his menu as the server approached. We ordered our food and a couple of Thai iced teas. Daniel played with his straw wrapper, which gave me license to inspect his hands again. He had the kind of fingernails I liked on a guy: clean, unbuffed, cut short.

"How did you get into that kind of work?" I asked. With a stab of anxiety, it crossed my mind that I had work of my own to do, but I told myself I'd get to it soon enough.

"In law school, I did an internship at the Kids Coalition and fell for public interest law. I started at the Foundation right out of law school and stayed. I just got appointed director of litigation."

Gorgeous, and a Good Samaritan to boot. I could swear he looked even hotter now that I knew what he did. "Congratulations!"

The restaurant was small, but packed, with every table full. The sounds of voices, clattering silverware, music, and occasional street noise reverberated off the hard walls and tables. We each leaned forward across the table to hear one another. His smile from afar had charmed me. His smile from a distance of six inches took my breath away.

He held out his tea glass to tap it against mine. "Cheers," he said.

I tapped back. "Cheers."

I marveled at myself, out to dinner with a really nice, attractive guy who acted perfectly happy to be here with me. Feeling like the heroine of my own romance, I gave him a flirtatious smile and looked coyly off to the side, only to catch sight of myself in a huge mirror with a ridiculous simper on my face and my hair all dented from the catcher's mask. I stopped smiling immediately and reminded myself that he was nice to everyone.

A plate of satay arrived—skewered strips of chicken with peanut sauce—and another with shrimp and vegetables. The server set the plates down to share between us, along with bowls of brown rice.

"So what did you call it—eating mindfully?" I asked him.

"Yeah," he said. "Take small bites. Savor each bite."

Following his example, I ate slowly, putting bits of shrimp and rice on my fork and noticing the blend of flavors and textures, enjoying the food while we talked. I sipped my tea, appreciating the sound of his voice through the faint buzz of alcohol. The world was a beautiful, interesting place, and for once, I belonged right in the middle of it, taking everything in.

Daniel told me he had no family except for his two brothers, twins, only one year younger. He was originally from Massachusetts and had gone to Brown, then moved out to UCLA, of all places, for law school. I felt a brief pang, thinking of Mark and wondering if he and Daniel would have known each other if Mark had gone to UCLA as planned. Daniel might have become a friend of ours instead of an accidental, quasi-date of mine.

"So what brought you to the program?" I asked.

"I started overeating when I was a kid," Daniel said. "Both my parents had died, and no one in the family wanted to take in three boys. The twins went to my aunt and uncle. I got farmed out to some distant cousins I didn't know. So food became my only friend."

I stared at him, horrified. His story was worse than mine.

He had started gaining weight in elementary school and was huge by the time he reached high school. "Imagine being fifteen and medically obese. Our PE coach used to torture me. If somebody did something wrong, Coach would yell out, 'Three laps around Daniel!'"

I caught my breath. "That's terrible."

He laughed ruefully. "I guess it's funny in a sick sort of way. Anyway, it's water under the bridge for me now."

"So the program really helped you?"

He nodded. "It's been amazing for me. It's not just the weight loss, either. It's everything. I feel good—at least, most of the time."

"I guess I should find a sponsor," I heard myself say, and I knew at that moment that if I committed to a sponsor, it wouldn't just be about going to New York or even my weight. It would be about me and reclaiming my life. I had to get myself going, and in the right direction.

"Michelle would be great for you," Daniel said.

"Do you sponsor people?"

"I sponsor guys. There are so few of us at the program. We tend to stick together." Another grin that sent me floating about an inch off the red plastic seat of the booth.

"You know," I said, "this eating mindfully isn't so bad. I kind of enjoyed it."

"Good!" He paused, then added, "Tonight was more fun than usual."

More eye contact, causing me to slide into a swoon. He leaned toward me again. "So what should I know about you?"

I thought for a second. All he knew so far was that I ate too much and worked for a man who belittled me. I needed to up my game. "Actually, I just signed my first book deal. My novel comes out in July."

He sat back. "Really? You're a published author?"

"Gonna be," I said, trying to put confidence into my voice. "Although it still doesn't seem real to me."

Daniel raised his eyebrows. "I'm impressed. Having a book published! And putting on a Hollywood premiere at the same time."

He was impressed! By me! I couldn't quite believe it.

"It's not as good as it sounds. You've seen what Josh is like." I told him how I'd wanted to be a writer all my life, how I wished I could stay home and write full time.

"I'd written a literary novel, but nobody was interested. I love romances, so I wrote one, which is the one that's being published."

"When does it come out?"

I had started to answer when a voice came from behind me.

"Daniel?"

Looking past me over my shoulder, Daniel tensed, his eyes dropping.

I turned around to see a woman in a red jacket, maybe thirty, hesitating and looking around, as if for an exit, then moving toward us, as if she'd decided escape was impossible. The scarf perfectly arranged around her neck, the freshly polished leather bag, and her smooth, sleek hair—all seemed at odds with her uncertain demeanor. "I'll meet you outside," she said to her companion, a woman who nodded and walked out the door.

"Rachel." Daniel's voice sounded suddenly hollow.

The woman stopped beside our table. I kept my mouth shut, and Daniel followed suit. An agonizingly long moment passed. She bit her lip, her face reddening.

"Are we still on . . ." Rachel finally said, "for tomorrow night?"

"Of course we're still on," Daniel said, shifting uncomfortably in his seat.

"Good then." She wavered, then crossed her arms and stood there.

"I'll pick you up tomorrow," Daniel said finally. His tone was meticulously polite, and yet her head jerked backward, as if he'd offended her. She nodded and headed off, her high heels making nervous little clicks on the tile floor.

Daniel hunched his shoulders and sighed. I couldn't tell if he was annoyed, embarrassed, or both.

"Awkward," I said. "Is that your girlfriend?"

He shook his head. "No! She's someone I've gone out with a few times in the last month."

"That's not very long," I said, trying to hide my relief as my mind registered the crucial information. *Not a girlfriend.*

"Long enough, it seems, for her to have gotten ideas." Daniel's fingers drummed the table.

"Oh."

"Yeah. Awkward." Distress wrinkled his forehead.

I leaped to reassure him. "Not all women have expectations. I mean, I wouldn't expect to be the only girl you're dating right now." I stopped. Somehow, that hadn't come out right. "Not that I think this is a date." Heat spread up my neck and cheeks.

Daniel was reaching for the check, his eyes fastened on the table.

"Let's split that." My insides were in a deep freeze of total mortification.

"Okay." He tossed some bills on the table and handed me the check. He didn't even look in my direction as I paid my half; instead, he checked the time on his cell phone and put on his jacket.

Good. By going dutch, we'd been clear. This was *not a date.*

I got an odd little pain in my throat.

He walked me to my car, said a quick goodbye, and took off, leaving me standing there.

I blinked back tears. The evening lay in pieces around me. I remembered I hadn't eaten very much for dinner. No way would

I have pigged out in front the only guy since Mark who had even slightly interested me.

Forget the program. My book changes could wait. I got into my car, turned on the ignition, and headed in the direction of the Frosty Foods drive-through. Right now, I needed a Jumbo Frosty Foods Chocolate Caramel Milkshake with all the toppings.

And maybe a large order of fries to go with it.

Twelve

The next morning, as I struggled out of bed, my mouth tasted sour and my stomach lurched. In my chest, the familiar pain of heartburn.

My planned milkshake and fries had turned into an epic, world-altering, excruciating eat-fest that had only been made worse by lack of sleep. My brain felt slow and stupid from staying up until 4:00 A.M. making changes for Kaitlyn.

I was convinced I'd gained an entire dress size since last night. Examining myself in the mirror revealed a waistline at least an inch bigger than it was yesterday. My face looked pale and bloated. And those ankles! They'd turned into cankles overnight.

Groaning, I started to get dressed. These pants had been looser the last time I wore them, I just knew it. I gritted my teeth as I fastened the button at the waist, sucking in my breath and pulling in my stomach. I couldn't afford to binge again.

And boy, did I want to.

Desperate, I skipped breakfast and brought a banana for lunch. By noon, famished and irritable, I decided I would need moral support if I ever hoped to get back on program. We were encouraged to call other program members in weak moments.

Josh lurked behind closed doors in his office, as usual. Line one was lit up, indicating I had a few minutes to myself.

Of course, I couldn't call Daniel after last night's debacle. But maybe . . . I picked up the phone.

"Hi! Michelle?"

"Sabrina, is that you?" In the background, the sounds of movement and small voices. "I'm with eight toddlers right now."

"Oh! I can call back later."

"I can talk for a minute. Someone's here helping."

"I was making an outreach call, but maybe this isn't a good time . . ."

A child's voice, then Michelle's. "Morgan, Robbie doesn't want you to draw on his arm." A piercing wail, followed by Michelle's voice. "I'm sorry. I have to take away your marker."

"Let's talk this weekend," I said, hanging up. Crap. In addition to talking cravings, I'd wanted to grill her about Daniel and this woman named Rachel. Now it would all have to wait at least two days, and I wanted to binge *now*.

I cast about for something to do besides eat. Surely my life included some opportunity for action more productive than shoveling down sweets.

Josh's phone line clicked off, causing my shoulders to hunch as I waited for him to emerge. But the light went on again—another reprieve. He'd been extra pissy lately as more and more time had passed, and Alexa Fredericks had still not returned the contract.

It bothered me. I couldn't believe Josh would give up that easily. No wonder he hadn't been able to attract any exciting new clients.

Alexa was a good actress. She needed to see that script he'd left behind. I'd read it, and it was wonderful.

If I brought it up to him, Josh would just yell at me, but I knew sending the script was worth a shot. He was letting a good opportunity slip away. He was acting like a loser, and I didn't want to work for a loser. Or be one.

Josh had long ago authorized me to write emails in his name, although the idea was that I would only do it with his knowledge. Deciding to dispense with that technicality, I opened a new email. He'd never know I'd done it, or if he found out, I'd just tell him he'd authorized it and didn't remember.

Alexa,

So great seeing you recently at Rinaldo's. I've taken the liberty of enclosing a wonderful, as-yet-undiscovered script titled Dead by Midnight. *I beg of you: read it at your earliest opportunity. This story has your name all over it. You would be the perfect Lenore—sassy, complex, and brilliant. It's a great opportunity for you, and only the first of many if you decide to join my agency.*

Please put me to work for you. Call me anytime with questions or concerns.

Josh Newman

Before I could chicken out, I attached the script and pressed send.

Although he didn't know it, Josh and I weren't out of the game yet.

On Saturday morning, Lena and I sat on the ledge of a low concrete wall that enclosed the landscaping in front of my apartment building. The shade from the trees overhead might have been pleasant had a bush not scratched and poked into my back. My cell phone lay on the wall beside me, as Kaitlyn was sending pages to review, and I had promised to do them all as soon as they came in. "You're so easy to work with!" she had enthused at me recently. "You get everything back to me fast and well done!"

"Thanks," I'd mumbled as dread trickled through me. Little did she know . . .

Why hadn't I told her the truth about the party right up front?

I shifted around, trying to find a comfortable spot on the hard ledge. Unfortunately, I wasn't expecting any calls from Daniel, who would likely never call me again after Wednesday's fiasco.

Stuart was changing the oil in my car, another skill of his that had appeared from nowhere after he went clean and sober. The black grease on his face and hands made him even handsomer than usual. He had stripped off his shirt, which had Lena fanning herself with her hand like a groupie. You'd think she'd get used to him since she lived with the guy and probably saw him naked every day.

Stuart lowered the hood of my car, which was parked at the curb a few steps away. "I'm done, Bree."

Who was cooler, him or Daniel? They were different, I decided. Stuart was a charming, laid-back Southern gentleman, whereas Daniel was this sexy combination of kind and considerate, yet really intense. The biggest difference, though, was Stuart totally belonged to Lena, whereas Daniel didn't belong to me even a little bit.

Lena got to her feet and approached her man. "You're getting grease in your hair! You should have tied it back." She rose on tiptoes to smooth his long hair behind his ears and gather it in a ponytail at the base of his neck.

As he looked down into her eyes, the electrical surge that passed between them could have knocked someone to the ground.

Lena's voice came out low and breathy. "Do you have a scrunchie?"

He touched his forehead to hers. "In my pocket."

More electricity as she slid her hand into the front pocket of his jeans.

Good grief. "Get a room, you two!" I vowed that if I ever fell in love again, I wouldn't be a total sap about it. I would keep my dignity.

My cell rang, flashing the name DANIEL. I nearly fell off my wall as I grabbed for it. "Hello, Daniel?" I was breathless, even though all I'd been doing was sitting, for Pete's sake.

"It's Michelle. I'm just using Daniel's phone, 'cause mine's charging."

"Oh, hi!" He must be nearby if she was using his phone.

"Sorry I couldn't talk the other day. But I've got time now."

I took a deep breath. "I'm doing really badly, Michelle. I'm bingeing, I'm gaining weight." It shocked me to realize I'd just told her the truth about my eating.

This was not the way I rolled. It was my lifelong pattern to lie about food.

Despite Michelle's silence, I could practically feel her warm sympathy flowing from the phone, surrounding me.

"I gotta do something to fix this . . . this mess I'm in."

"You want a sponsor?"

"Really? You'd be willing to do that?"

"I'd be honored."

Regret washed over me as I thought of my romp that had begun with french fries and a milkshake and had ended two days later with a large meat-lover's pizza and a box of Milk Duds. Yet another setback to overcome.

"You feel ready to start the steps?"

"I guess so. I have to make amends, right?"

"That comes later. You're at Step One, where you admit that you've lost control of your eating and your life."

Let's see, where should I start? Perhaps with the incident where I'd been found on the floor of the reception area eating Oreos on my hands and knees. "I think I could say that I've lost control of my eating and my life." I glanced over at the lovebirds, who were laughing and whispering in each other's ears.

"I'll give you some readings, which we'll talk about," Michelle said. "And when you're ready, we'll go to Step Two."

"What's that?"

"It's where you come to believe that a power greater than yourself can bring order to your life."

This comment brought me to a screeching halt. "Yeah. About the higher power thing, I'm a bit weak in that area." This program was too weird for me. *Face it,* I told myself, *you'd have been out of this a long time ago if the New York trip weren't looming over your head. And if Daniel weren't so adorable.*

I suddenly realized that Stuart and Lena had stopped talking and were openly listening to my end of the conversation. "Could we talk about this another time?"

"Sure," Michelle said. "What about Monday? We could meet at five thirty at the Coffee Station and go straight to a meeting afterward."

"Great!"

"Just do one thing for me this weekend, before we meet. Eat three healthy meals each day and email me a list of your food. Will you do that?"

"Okay . . ." I hesitated. "Y-Yes, I will. Where are you, anyway? Why are you calling on Daniel's phone?"

"I'm at home. Daniel's here. He and James are leaving on a hike soon."

"Tell them hello."

"Say hi yourself."

And then Daniel was on the line, his voice completely normal, as if we hadn't had that embarrassing moment a few days ago. "Hey, Bree. You're going to the Monday night meeting with Michelle?"

"I guess so, yeah."

"I'll see you then!"

I hung up, thinking maybe there was, in fact, a higher power looking out for me. I mean, how else could this totally hot, interesting man have dropped from nowhere into my life? Even though we absolutely, positively weren't dating. Slowly, my gaze refocused itself onto my sister and her guy.

"So . . . Step Two, huh?" A broad grin crossed Stuart's face. "That's a tough one. I helped Leenie with that one." He slipped his arm around her waist.

"Really, how?"

He and Lena exchanged glances. "You want us to show you?"

"Um, maybe." I looked back and forth between them.

"It'll be fun. Or . . . let's say it'll be interesting."

"I guess. Yes."

"Good," Stuart said. "We'll pick you up tomorrow at five A.M."

"Five A.M.! Forget it."

"Come on, start the day early," Stuart drawled. "It'll be good for you!"

"I'll pull you out of bed if I have to." Lena shot me a stern look.

"All right, all right." I sighed. I didn't know where I was going, but I was going.

Thirteen

Stuart and I stood at the edge of the ocean with our surfboards. In the early morning light, the water was a menacing flat gray, the color of approaching doom. My fear of drowning was exceeded only by the fear of having my corpulent remains seen in a borrowed wet suit. I'd be humiliated even in death.

"Are there sharks out there?" I consoled myself with the idea that, if I got eaten, there'd be no body to recover. I would be remembered solely by my hot website picture, which would run over the headline, Local Beauty Consumed by Shark.

"Not very often," Stuart answered, his eyes appraising the waves. He exuded a sort of bliss, as if his mind were entering a state of nirvana.

"How often is 'not very often'?" My mewling voice grated against the morning silence. "I mean, is it once a year? Once a month? Every morning?" The water rushed hard over my legs, gushing past me, then pulling the sand out from under my feet as it retreated.

"Shhh." Stuart shushed me gently, as if I were a small child, and raised a hand to the heavens. "Be ready to receive the experience!"

I would kill Lena. I had assumed she would do this with us, but no, she had dropped us at the beach and taken off with Twinkie. "He needs a walk," she'd told me, as if that were an excuse for abandoning her older sister to a watery fate. "And besides, I've already done Step Two."

"Body centered on the board," Stuart instructed. "As we paddle toward the wave, keep the tip of the board up."

I clambered atop the board, hitting it with a smack and clinging to it crosswise, which was all wrong. Within two arm strokes, I had tumbled off into the surf. Stinging salt water entered my nose as I came up gasping for air. I struggled to plant my feet on the ocean floor and finally stood for a moment in the shallow surf, catching my breath, while a couple of seagulls mocked me from the air.

"Try again."

"I am, I am!" I'd always been a strong swimmer. Despite my fear, I felt a spark of interest. Pushing against the moving water, I climbed onto the board again, making sure I was halfway back and centered the way Stuart had told me.

"Good," Stuart said. "Now paddle hard with your arms and head straight out toward and over the wave. Keep your tip up!"

I paddled, but the surfboard's tip went into the wave, pulling both it and me under. As the water boiled around me, I thrashed, completely disoriented, holding my breath and trying to find my way up. Seeing light, I shot in its direction, thinking, *I got this!* I broke the surface but could do no more than gasp before a second wave tossed me sideways.

Just stand up, I told myself. If it had been still, the water would have been waist-high, but it wasn't still. In fact, I'd never been in surf this rough. The ocean seemed possessed. It heaved as a series of new waves reached me. I fought to regain my footing in the sand, but a third wave hit me, then a fourth, each one engulfing me for a brief moment and knocking me off my feet. My nose and mouth filled with salty water, and I spat it out, trying to breathe. A fifth wave picked me up like a toy and dragged me under.

A hand grabbed my wrist and pulled, hard, helping me up and onto the beach, above the reach of the waves. "You okay?" Stuart asked.

I nodded, bending over with my hands on my knees, hacking and spitting seawater. My eyes burned and my nose dripped.

"Sorry. That was a little intense," he said, thumping my back.

I gagged in response. "Is it always like this?"

"Pretty much. You get used to it." He spoke in a voice of quiet triumph. "Anyway. You've just experienced a power far greater than yourself."

Given that I'd practically died in four feet of water, I was inclined to believe him.

"So, let's give it another shot!" he said.

Since in my mind being fat ordinarily trumped any possible athletic talent I had, I tended to forget how much I liked sports. For the next hour, though, as Stuart and I practiced paddling out over the waves, I was having so much fun that I'd forgotten to be embarrassed about my body in a wet suit. We did it over and over again until I was getting it right every time.

We had just passed over a series of waves and were farther out than we'd ever gone. I was breathing heavily. My arms and legs glowed warm from the exercise, protecting me from the cold wind and the sunless morning sky.

"Follow me!" Stuart paddled a bit farther to flat water and motioned to me to stop. We sat, straddling our surfboards, bobbing peacefully, and looking at the shore. A lot of surfers milled about at the water's edge, but we were alone out here.

"You did really well!" Stuart said. "Great, for a beginner."

"Thanks!" I wondered if we could do it again sometime. Or maybe I'd sign up for lessons this summer. But that would mean

I'd have to be seen in a bathing suit, which could not be allowed to happen.

I peered over at Stuart, who leaned back on his arms, eyes closed, face to the sky.

"This," he said, "is God."

"What is?"

"This. All of it." Stuart opened his eyes and looked at me. "It's like, God is the ocean, a force a million times more powerful than me. And my life is in these waves he's sending toward me. Some are scary and dangerous, and others are cool and fun, and I can ride all of them. But to do that, I gotta obey the waves. I gotta go where they take me."

"And if you don't?"

He put a thumb down. "*Wipeout!*"

I grinned, loving his metaphor. "So that's you, huh, just surfing along on the wave of life?"

"Something like that." His face veiled over. "Are you laughing at me?" He sat up straight on his surfboard.

"No! Stuart!" I shook my head, my salty hair slapping my cheeks. "I loved what you just said!"

We looked at each other for a moment, our boards going up and down—first mine, then his as each wave passed.

"I'm glad we did this," I said. "I'm glad you're with Lena. She's happy."

He nodded, two spots of new color on his cheeks. The wind picked up, and I shivered. Thunderclouds were gathering overhead.

"Let's head in," Stuart said.

Lena waited for us beside the car holding two paper cups. "Hot chocolate. It may seem weird in May, but I don't care. That water's cold in the morning!"

I warmed my hands on the cup and sipped the chocolate. I almost moaned it was so good. After two hours of hard practice, I'd earned this. I clutched the paper cup and took another sip, savoring it, while reminding myself to add it to my food diary for Michelle.

Standing in a parking lot by the Pacific Ocean, covered with sand, warm from exercise yet cold from the water, laughing as Stuart described to Lena my tumbling through the surf—I felt a strange longing that every day could be like this. No hiding in my room, no obsessing over what and when I would eat again—just moving my body, enjoying the wind against my face, and hanging with people I loved.

Lena slipped her arm around me, her soft hair brushing my cheek. "How was it? Did you have a spiritual awakening?"

"I dunno about that, but I had fun!"

"She's a natural," Stuart told Lena. "We should go again, the three of us. Next weekend?"

"I'm in!" Now that I could paddle out, I was dying to see if I could catch a wave.

We piled into Stuart's giant 1964 Lincoln Continental, with Lena, Stuart, and Twinkie up front and me alone in the back seat. I usually didn't mind being their third wheel, but today I thought of Daniel, half wishing he were here. It would be nice to think that I might start to date again, that I might begin seeing Daniel, and that once again, just maybe, I might be ready to fall in love.

But first, I had to lose those forty pounds.

Fourteen

On Monday, my advance check arrived at the office by messenger. Four thousand dollars! I kissed it. I'd never seen anything so beautiful.

I would use money to make myself presentable for my New York trip. A nice dress for evening events and something tailored yet fashionable for day. I knew my long hair was good. I would spruce it up with layers and professional highlights instead of my usual do-it-yourself-over-the-bathroom-sink job. And my nails! No long acrylic nails; instead, I'd wear them neat and short with sophisticated dark polish. Finally, with whatever was left, I would pay off a tiny part of my mountain of debt. Such things were now within my reach, because of this one incredible slip of paper.

I wasn't hungry, so it was simply force of habit that set me to rustling through my food drawer. I unearthed a Kit Kat bar, automatically looking forward to the crunch of wafer and creamy sweetness of chocolate.

I stopped myself. Over the weekend, I had not only wrestled the Pacific Ocean, but I'd managed to eat the three healthy meals a day that Michelle had requested. I had emailed her my food list both days in return for smiley-faced responses.

So far I hadn't lied to her, but that would all change if I started in with the Kit Kats.

That didn't feel good. It wasn't the lying itself that bothered me. For me, lying about food was part of my fundamental right to privacy, not to mention a way of thumbing my nose at the haters. Haters were the naturally thin people who dared to look down on fat people, when the only difference between them and us was that they could hide their sins and weaknesses, while we had to wear them for everyone to see.

But Michelle wasn't one of those people. She was trying to help me. I would see her this evening at the Coffee Station before the meeting, and I wanted to be able to tell her truthfully that I'd done something right.

With a sigh, I pulled out my paper lunch bag and peeked in. Celery sticks. An apple. A turkey sandwich.

Maybe it was close enough to lunchtime that I could justify eating my sandwich. Say, ten o'clock. With that hopeful thought, I checked my little desk clock.

Nine thirty. I'd been in the office for fifteen minutes. It was a late start for me, but concern for Josh had kept me awake half the night, emailing out the last of the invitations and combing through our guest list to be sure no one who mattered had been forgotten.

What did that speaker say at the last meeting? We ate to numb feelings like sorrow, boredom, anger, fear. If you wanted to stop the crazy eating, you had to be able to live with that discomfort. You had to learn to ride out the feelings until they went away.

I poured myself a glass of water and studied my to-do list through bleary eyes. I would replace eating with productive activity. Although it didn't sound like much fun, it was better than becoming a beluga whale.

I had come to the Coffee Station many times when I was writing *Passion*. It was one of those rare you-can-sit-forever coffee places that did not belong to an international chain. It featured gingham curtains, pots of sunflowers, and the owner's homemade blueberry muffins and crumb cake, which I'd enjoyed back when I allowed myself to partake of such things.

I sat in a booth near the front so Michelle and I could find each other easily. I needn't have worried, as her royal-purple and acid-green track suit practically glowed against the dark wood paneling when she walked in. I contemplated the awfulness of her latest fashion choice. She looked like a giant extra-ripe eggplant.

I laughed to myself, then flushed with shame. What was wrong with me, anyway? Michelle was a lovely person, and it wasn't like I was such a great dresser. I knew that wasn't the most important thing.

Weird how I was starting to realize I wasn't always the kindest person. It was disconcerting, since I'd always thought that, except for being fat, of course, I was quite a decent sort. All I had to do was lose the fat—right?—and everything, including me, would be great.

Over our tea and Greek salads, I committed to eating three nutritious, moderately sized meals every day, plus two fruit snacks. I would email my food to Michelle daily along with a list of five things I was grateful for. I would go to four meetings a week and call Michelle every Monday, Wednesday, and Friday at 10:15 A.M.

"One more thing," Michelle said.

Was she kidding? What else could there be?

"I need you to take a job," she said. "Like new member rep. Or greeter. We swap them out every six months."

"These are weird requirements for a diet," I grumbled.

"It's not a diet. It's . . . how can I say this? The program helps you change yourself and revise your mistaken thinking and behavior. Then, you can stop overeating and hurting yourself." Michelle brought her napkin to her lips and pushed her plate away.

"If this program's so great, how come everyone's not doing it?"

"It's hard work. Plus, we don't advertise. People hear about us and come to us when they're ready."

"I don't know if I'm ready. I don't know about this spiritual stuff. You know, God and all that."

Michelle shrugged. "That keeps a lot of people away. Like me. I only came because I'd hit rock bottom. I was completely desperate." She picked up the check and looked it over. "You don't have to do this, you know. But we're here if you ever are ready."

"No, I'll try! If you'll work with me."

She sat back. "Sure. If you're interested, I'm in."

Was I really ready to buckle down and work through my problems? Or was this just about getting skinny to please my editor? Or was it really about a guy with bright blue eyes? Who, I reminded myself, seemed to be dating someone else.

Michelle sat beside me at the meeting as we listened to a woman named Marcy share. "The program book says that we are inextricably linked to the people we resent. During Step Four, I came up with eighty-seven things my ex had said and done that I still held against him. No wonder I couldn't move on from my marriage!"

I bet I could come up with eighty-seven resentments against my parents. Against my mother for abandoning us, for every birthday, holiday, and graduation ignored. Against my father for all the nights we waited, hungry, for him to come home late from work with food for the house. For all the school events he missed, the sleepovers and parties he couldn't take us to. Funny, I kind of enjoyed my anger against them, in a sick sort of way. If I let it go, what would I do with all my negative energy?

Michelle glanced over at me a couple of times during Marcy's share. As usual, I kept my hand down.

"You didn't want to share?" she asked as the meeting ended.

"Not my style." No way was I going to blab all over these people about my private stuff. I headed into the linoleum-floored hallway, Michelle beside me.

She made a face. "I want you to share at the next meeting you go to."

"No thanks."

"Sponsor's orders."

I stuck my tongue out at her. "Okay, but . . . not if Daniel's there." We started down the stairs.

Michelle made a *tsk* noise. "That shouldn't make a difference. Anyway, you guys should get to know each other. You'd like each other."

"Is that why you left us to have dinner alone the other night?" We had reached the sidewalk outside the churchyard.

"I don't know what you're talking about." Michelle's eyes crinkled up at the corners.

I stopped walking. "What's the story with that girl Rachel?"

Michelle hesitated, as if deciding what she wanted to say. "They've gone out a few times. I think Daniel likes her okay, but she's a little clingy."

"He talks to you about stuff like that?" I couldn't see him exchanging heartfelt confidences with Michelle.

Michelle shook her head. "No. He plays his cards pretty close to his chest. But we went out with them once."

"What's she like?"

"She's fine, I guess. I shouldn't talk about her." Michelle patted my arm. "Lemme just say that Daniel's a good guy, worth getting to know. Whatever details you need, get them from him."

Darn it. Just when things could have gotten interesting, my information source ran dry. "Here's my car," I said.

"We're gonna do another softball game," Michelle said. "Wanna come? It's next Wednesday."

"Sure!" Softball on Wednesday, surfing on Saturday. I was becoming a jock without even trying.

My cell rang. Josh again. "What is it?" I didn't care if I sounded impatient. Why was he bugging me at eight o'clock at night?

"Sabrina?" His voice cracked, and he breathed heavily, as if he'd been running. "Get over here. I'm at home."

An alarm began to ring in my head. "Is everything okay?"

"I need you. Now!"

I blurted my goodbyes to Michelle and, with quick, careful motions, entered Josh's home address into my GPS. I'd never been to his house, never had a reason to go, and didn't know why I was being summoned now. Worried, clueless about what could be wrong, I drove as fast as I could through the heavy traffic.

Fifteen

In the Beverly Hills flats, where Josh and Corinne lived, I was sure the streets had been designed by sadists. They were quiet, straight residential streets that appeared to be long, and therefore, just the place to go pedal to the metal. That is, until you hit the first stop sign . . . and then the second . . . and then the third. Trying to respond to Josh's emergency, I alternated for nine blocks between flooring the gas and slamming on the brakes, guzzling my way through probably half a tank of gasoline and dislodging a dozen vertebrae. Finally, I pulled into the driveway of Josh's mansion, a replica of a southern plantation, complete with a veranda and two-story columns. To the left was an enormous Spanish-style hacienda; to the right, a sleek, white contemporary number with green-glass and matte-chrome finishes.

The front door opened, and Josh stepped out, car keys in hand.

His face sagged. His skin had turned a putty gray. One side of his shirt collar, instead of slipping neatly under his jacket lapel, had gotten caught and stuck straight up into the air.

He didn't waste any time. "The day nurse went home sick, and Corinne's missing."

"Missing!"

"It's never happened before." His hands shook. "I'm going to look for her, but I need someone . . . I needed someone

I knew would come . . ." He swallowed and stared off for a second. "Someone I can, you know, trust to handle things, in case she comes home or calls. If she does, would you keep her here and phone me *immediately*?"

Startled by this new Josh I'd never seen, I gave an automatic reply. "Of course."

He pointed me into the foyer and took off, leaving me with a million unanswered questions. Like, for example, why call me? I got that he was upset by Corinne's disappearance, but couldn't he and his wife work out their own problems, or turn to friends or family? Maybe not. He'd as much as admitted he needed my help, for the first time ever in the history of my indentured servitude to him. It left me confused, but with a little warm spot, nonetheless.

Alone with nothing to do, I stared up at the two-story marble-lined atrium that served as the entry to his home. I moved into the living room and wandered around, eyeing the Persian rugs and fancy little urns and figurines. There were paned windows framed with incredibly heavy-looking floor-to-ceiling curtains. I ran my finger down the rich, green velvet, noticing letters in gold thread: JSN. CAN.

Having applied for the personalized license plates on their cars, I recognized the letters as their initials. JSN—Joshua Seymour Newman. CAN—Corinne Aurelia Newman.

The Newmans sure did like to monogram their stuff. Sofa cushions, guest towels in the powder room, the welcome mat outside the front door—all bore the initials JSN or CAN. I found it a bit much but reminded myself it wasn't my business.

Both the day and the room were getting dark, thus curtailing my snooping. I found a bank of wall switches and flicked a few, then jumped as Bruce Springsteen blasted through unseen speakers while the curtains rustled together and closed. Oops. Trying to turn off Bruce, I accidentally ignited the gas fireplace, but eventually got rid of both the music and the fire and managed to turn on a few lights. The curtains wouldn't reopen no matter what I tried. Since it was dark outside, I figured it was okay to leave them closed.

Too nervous to sit down, I continued my wanderings, ending up in their five-star kitchen. I admired the sand-colored granite, the stainless-steel appliances, the large windows, and the huge island holding a silver bowl, engraved with their initials and piled high with peaches. Not that I would actually use a kitchen like this. From my obsession with eating, one might think I would, but no. I did not store, prepare, or cook food; I just ate it.

What did they keep in their pantry? One ear cocked for the sound of a returning car, I tiptoed to a wall of louvered folding doors and slid one open.

A binger's dream. Crackers, chips, nuts, and trail mixes, at least a half dozen kinds of cookies, a jumbo container of chocolate-dipped biscotti, and two boxes of See's Candies.

Now, this was the funny thing about food obsession. In the face of such bounty, all thoughts of the program and commitments to my sponsor flew instantly from my head. I thought of it as opportunity eating. You took food when and where you found it, not because you were hungry or wanted it, not because it belonged to you or you had any right to it, but because it was there.

I'd never thought about it much before or questioned it; it was just what I did. But it was, I suddenly realized, pretty strange behavior. In fact, it was addict behavior.

Putting that thought aside, I peered around for security cameras. So long as I wasn't caught on film, they would never know a few handfuls had gone missing from their pantry. I inspected the packages.

The key was to take only a little, and just from opened packages. One of the See's boxes was open, as well as a bag of barbecue potato chips, and six other packages of cookies and assorted treats. Still listening for Josh's arrival, I laid my pilfered goods on a paper towel—a few chips, a chocolate truffle, two cookies, a mini bran muffin, and a handful of kettle corn—then stopped to admire my spread.

But then, a strange thing happened.

Michelle's voice in my ear. *Count to ten.*

The idea was to buy yourself some time, to slow down, calm down, invite your brain into a quiet place, where you could think.

One. Breathe. Slow and calm.

Two. Ten didn't seem like enough. Maybe I should count to fifty.

Three. At a distance, a key turned in a lock.

Saved. Moving as fast as I could, I replaced the lid on the box of See's. The front door opened, and footsteps sounded on the marble floors of the foyer. Hands shaking, I refastened the clips on bags of chips and kettle corn. A female voice crooned too softly for me to catch the words, but then I heard the click of toenails on the floor and the jingle of metal tags. She had a dog with her. My heart thumped as I closed up the last boxes and shoved them into the pantry, sliding the door with an audible click.

"Is someone there?" The woman's voice had an edge to it now.

Not even a moment to mourn the loss of my delicious goodies. I gathered up my paper towel into a little sack and burrowed it down into the trash, then whirled around, my hands behind my back, shutting the garbage drawer with my body.

"I'm Sabrina. I work for your husband." I blurted the words, hoping she wouldn't be scared.

The woman stood in the archway leading in from the dining room. A thinner, paler version of the photos in Josh's office, she had to be Corinne. She stared at me. Her perfect features would have been beautiful had she not been completely expressionless, with dark shadows curved under her eyes. She wore a nondescript sweatshirt over a pair of jeans, casual wear that contrasted sharply with the glittering diamonds on both of her hands. She held the leash of a large standard poodle, who wagged his tail tentatively at the sight of me.

I kept talking, trying to calm any fears that she might have. "Josh wasn't sure where you were. He asked me to stay here while he went out looking for you."

She regarded me for a second. "I spoke to you on the phone, didn't I?"

"Yes." Uh-oh. She was going to ask me about the bracelet.

She looked around, then spoke in a low voice, as if she were telling me a secret. "I couldn't tell you the other day, but Josh had already given me the bracelet."

She'd had it all along? I couldn't help but be a little pissed off. She'd scared me half to death with that story. "Why couldn't you tell me?"

"You know why." She walked over and peered down a dark hall-way, her back to me. Over her shoulder, she said, "The same reason you shut the curtains in the living room."

"Beg your pardon?"

"The same reason I saved Prometheus." She nodded down at the poodle, who stood close by her side and now sniffed her shoe.

"Prometheus?" A shiver ran through me. Why was she staring down that hallway? Was someone there?

Her voice rose. "Our neighbor's dog, silly! They were going to take him."

Corinne was certainly a bit unusual. Her breath was starting to come in little gasps. "You know all about them. I can tell—you shut the curtains." She gave me an approving look.

I remembered the line from *Alice's Adventures in Wonderland*: "Curiouser and curiouser."

"I know all about who?"

"The Lawn People." Her hands fluttered through the air. "The ones who spy through the windows. Who listen on the phones!" The last words came out in a frightened whisper.

The front door flew open, and Josh burst in, bringing a wave of cold air with him. "Cor, I looked all over for you!" He gathered her up in his arms. "Where were you? I keep telling you, you've gotta take your medications!"

Corinne clutched her husband's lapels. "Sabrina sees them too. She knows. She shut the curtains!"

His arms still around his wife, Josh turned his head in my direction. I'd never seen him in a state like this: tender, relieved, grieving, and completely beside himself. No wonder he seemed unbalanced at work sometimes.

He threw me a despairing look. "When did she get back?"

"Just now. Do you need anything else?" I asked, hoping the answer was no.

"We're fine."

"*Fine?* The Lawn People are coming!" Corinne clung to Josh, her hands on his chest. "Sabrina knows! She understands. She fortified the house against them!"

Josh shot me a look of pure weariness, which I could only answer with a helpless shrug. As his arms tightened around Corinne, she began to struggle. "I've got to go, Josh. I've got to hide from them."

"Cor, do you remember what we said about the Lawn People?" Josh's voice was a heartbreaking mixture of gentle and exhausted. "Those are the people whose voices only you can hear."

"Only I can hear?" Corinne's eyes brimmed with doubt.

Looking at her small, vulnerable face, I felt sorry for her. She lived in a frightening world that no one else saw or believed in.

"Yeah, remember? It means the Lawn People aren't real. If only you can hear a certain person, and others can't, that person isn't real."

For the first time, he seemed to focus on Prometheus. "What's that dog doing here?"

Suddenly defiant, Corinne faced off against her husband. "I saved him."

"You . . . ?" Josh's eyes widened in alarm. "Did you take that dog?" He didn't stop for an answer. "Wait a minute. Is that *Pamela Wellman's* dog?"

He knelt to study the tags on the dog's collar, causing the poodle to lunge forward to lick his face. "No, quit that!" He held the dog off. Prometheus retreated for a moment before he surged back toward Josh again, tail wagging.

"The Lawn People wanted to hurt him. I just moved him to a safe place."

"It *is* hers!" Josh let the tag in his hand fall, jingling. "That woman already wants to put my nuts in a vise over all this!"

Corinne drew herself up, her eyes flashing a stormy pale gray. "She'll *appreciate* the fact that I *cared* enough to remove her dog from a dangerous environment. She should know better than to leave him alone outside."

"And where, exactly, was he?"

A moment of silence, then, Corinne's answer in a haughty voice. "His backyard."

Her husband stared at her in horror. "You *stole* him?"

"No! He followed me out." Corinne hunched her shoulders, dropping her eyes. "I might have put one of our old leashes on him . . . from when we had Duchess."

"Oh, *man!*" Drops of sweat popped onto Josh's brow as he began to pace. "She'll fuckin' *crucify* me!"

He wheeled in my direction. "Sabrina! I need you to put him back."

"*What?*" Josh was just as crazy as Corinne. "Josh! I can't do that!"

"It's easy." Josh rapped out staccato instructions. "Our houses are back-to-back, right across the alley from each other. You go out our back gate with Fido here, cross the alley, open Pamela's back gate, and . . . presto chango! The dog's home."

"Can't *you* do it?" But seeing Josh's paleness and the unsteadiness of his hands, I experienced a sinking feeling of inevitability.

Josh was herding us through the kitchen and out a sliding door onto a covered patio. Nearby, a pool gleamed a serene aqua, while a stone path veered left, disappearing behind a boxwood hedge. Prometheus, who seemed to have grasped Josh's agenda, led the way, pulling along a complaining Corinne, while I followed, protesting even more loudly than she was. As we stumbled along, Josh, at the rear, peppered me with explanations.

"She's already threatened to get a restraining order."

I gave him a questioning look.

"Because Corinne put piles of salt in her driveway . . . to ward off evil spirits."

"Not that she was even *slightly* inconvenienced by a little rock salt," Josh went on in a bitter voice, "but still, Pamela made this giant stink about it and doesn't want Corinne anywhere near her house." Josh continued close behind me, panting in my ear. "Me either, for that matter. That's why I need *you* to put the dog back."

"So I can be arrested instead of you? Can't Corinne just say it was an honest mistake?"

"Mistake?" Corinne bristled. "I *helped* her!"

"*Please,* Sabrina? You won't be arrested," Josh said. "She'd recognize me or Cor if she saw us, but she doesn't know you. And anyway, she won't see you. In and out. Two minutes. That's all it'll take."

I stood at the Newmans' back gate, leash in hand, cursing my existence. Josh had persuaded his wife to let Prometheus return home. Now I peered into the darkened alley, trying to see across to Pamela Wellman's back gate. The large poodle, knowing home was near, strained at the leash, pulling me forward.

"She probably doesn't even know the dog's gone yet," Josh wheedled from behind me. "If you do it fast, you'll be fine!"

Hoping for the best, I stumbled across, following Prometheus to a door, where he stopped, looking up at me expectantly. The numbers on the door confirmed it was the right one. *Thank goodness,* I thought, reaching for the doorknob. Corinne had said it would be open.

It was locked.

I tried it several times, unable to believe my bad luck. It remained stubbornly closed against us. Prometheus whined and scratched at the door, then let loose with a volley of barks, registering his outrage.

"C'mon, boy!" I raced back across the alley, pulling the dog with me and reaching Josh's door.

It was locked too.

I pounded on the door, no longer caring about noise. "Josh, let me in!"

His voice came from behind the door: "Please just return the dog first?"

"*Let. Me. In!*"

"Just tell her you found him. I can't afford to have her know we were involved."

I looked over toward Pamela's dark, still backyard. No sign that she'd missed her beloved pet yet or was up looking for him. Her wall had to be seven feet high. No way to get myself over it, let alone a big dog.

"*Josh!*" This time I kicked his door, only to be greeted by silence.

I wanted to kill Josh for this. At the same time, I knew I could do it. Already, a plan was forming in my head.

Standing next to me in the dark, Prometheus gave a tentative whimper and put his cold nose in my hand.

"It's okay, boy. I won't leave you."

All I had to do was return the dog without implicating Josh and Corinne. I would figure out what to say to Pamela when I got there.

By now, Prometheus really wanted his dinner. He galloped down the alley, pulling me behind him as I counted the houses passing by. There were five between his house and the side street. When we reached the street, I was able to slow him to a fast walk. We made a right, then another right, then counted the houses again as the dog towed me up his street in the direction we'd come.

The sixth house. This was it. A Colonial-style brick home with wrought iron and painted shutters. I wanted to stop and catch my breath, but Prometheus tore up the front walk, his toenails scrabbling on the flagstone, unable to contain his excitement.

As he reached the front steps, the door flew open. A leggy woman strode down the stairs, arms open, a vision in a brown pantsuit, white blouse, and little brown scarf tied around her neck. I giggled to myself over her short, bowl-shaped haircut.

She scuffled lovingly with the poodle, who jumped on her, clawing at her clothing. "Prom, you old rascal! Thank goodness you're okay!"

My internal giggles stopped short when she leveled her gaze on me. "Who are you?" It was the second time this evening that I'd been asked that question.

Time to earn my salary. "Are you Pamela Wellman? I found your dog on the street. I didn't want him to get hurt, so I brought him home to you."

"Well, thank you! I was about to hang signs, but they wouldn't have done much good in the dark." She grimaced and ruffled her dog's ears.

"Anyway," I said, "I'd better be going." This was going to be a piece of cake. I congratulated myself on my cleverness.

"No, wait!" She seemed to search for the right thing to say. "I really owe you. Would you like to come in?"

My reply was immediate and heartfelt. "No. I'm just glad I could help."

"Well, at least take your leash." She unclipped it from the dog's collar.

Oh, right. Corinne's leash. As I held out my hand for it, my eyes fell on the monogrammed letters CAN in black on silver near the looped handle. Seeing Pamela squint in the direction of the incriminating evidence, I put my hand over it and snatched the leash away from her.

She stared at me for a moment, then asked, "How'd you know where my dog lived?"

"I read his tags." I gave a cheery wave. "Goodbye!"

"My name and address aren't on the tags. Just my phone number."

"Oh, yes, of course. I just followed Prometheus home." I started down the steps.

"Okay. But where'd you get this leash?"

"Um . . . Canada. Oops, that's my phone! Gotta go!"

Canada? Could I have been any more stupid?

Panicking, I sprinted off into the darkness. I didn't dare look back.

Josh didn't come into the office the next day, but instead left a brief voicemail telling me to postpone all appointments for the week and await further instructions. The time of the message was 3:00 A.M. He didn't mention our misadventure with Pamela and Prometheus, but his message was probably left before Pamela would have called him.

I would just have to hope I'd been wrong about her seeing Corinne's initials on the leash.

By noon, I had rearranged Josh's calendar, soothed the ruffled feathers of the more high-maintenance clients, handled those things I could do on my own, and noted a few things to run by Josh when he called in. There was nothing left to do except sit here and answer the phone.

It didn't ring. I inspected my nails and reorganized a few files. Normally, I'd jump at the chance to brainstorm ideas for my next book, since I'd finished my changes on this one, but today my mind kept going back to Josh.

I wondered what he was doing today, how Corinne was, whether he was getting help for her. I had never thought about what his life must be like, the problems that he had.

Now there didn't seem to be just one way for me to feel about Josh. The image of him speaking patiently to the frightened wife in his arms made my heart feel open and mushy, a new and not entirely comfortable sensation. On the other hand, the fact that he'd seen fit last night to push me into a dark alley and lock the door against me made me feel a bit less charitable.

I thought about Daniel, who was always around and yet so frustratingly unavailable. I thought about New York and how unprepared I was, and how my dream of getting published had turned into a nightmare that was all about how I looked and not how I wrote.

And then, an ice-cream sandwich loomed into my imagination, the kind with vanilla ice cream between two giant chocolate chip cookies. The ice cream was just starting to get soft. The cookies looked chewy, but tender, studded with the perfect ratio of chocolate chips to cookie dough. My mouth began to water.

I was starting my fourth day of mindful eating and had planned to go out for a salad at lunchtime. The problem was, I hadn't emptied out my food drawer yet. There was a brand-new jumbo bag of peanut M&M's in there and a new box of Ho Hos. A siren song floated from the drawer's interior: *Food, glorious food!*

I couldn't do it. I couldn't go rogue on my fourth day. It was too lame, even for me. It would force me to lie to Michelle, which would make me feel like dirt, but would still be better than how I'd feel if I told her the truth. Theoretically, I should be calling her for help, but instead I called Lena. "Can you come to my office?"

"What's wrong?"

"Food emergency!"

Twenty minutes later, I heard Lena out in the reception area.

"Bree, where are you?"

I sat curled up in one of the big armchairs in Josh's office. I'd shut the door and put my fingers in my ears, but I still heard the food song in my head. "Lena!" I croaked from my chair.

The door opened. "What is all this?" Lena nodded her head back to the reception area.

I had barricaded my desk drawer shut with a filing cabinet that I'd barely managed to push into place. My theory was that later on, when my resolve died and I tried to move the cabinet away to get my sweets back, I'd be too weak from hunger to do it. But now, I realized even that wasn't good enough. I needed bigger guns. "Ho Hos! In my food drawer!"

As the experienced significant other of a recovering drug addict, Lena didn't miss a beat.

"I'm on it!"

While I cowered in Josh's office, little Lena somehow found the strength to push the file cabinet away from my desk. The rustling of cellophane, footsteps on carpet, the sound of the door, then silence. I sat there and mourned for my vanished sweets. Would I ever eat a piece of chocolate again? How would I survive?

The door opened once more, and Lena was back with a smug look on her face. "That was fun."

"For you," I moaned, burying my face in Josh's sofa cushions.

"Take deep breaths." My sister sat down across from me in an armchair. She wore a little tank dress with her hair pulled back in a ponytail, in keeping with the warm day outside but not my air-conditioned office. "Slowly. In and out. In and out."

I needed a change of subject. "I met Josh's wife. She's crazy." I felt bad speaking that way about Corinne but figured my sister wouldn't hold it against me.

"We're all a little bit crazy." Lena hugged herself, rubbing her arms for warmth.

"No, I mean seriously mentally ill." I told her the whole story. "Josh is taking the rest of the week off to deal with it."

"Wow, poor guy."

Words I would never have applied to Josh before. "I know. So, thanks for coming. You weren't doing anything, were you?"

I'd expected a no. Lena usually wasn't doing much. But this time, she brightened. "I just finished a job interview."

"Really? With who?"

Two spots of color appeared on her cheeks. "It's actually a good job—working as an assistant for Olivia Landers." She gave me a tentative smile. "I really liked temping for her, and I think she liked me."

The caterer. It reminded me that Olivia wanted me to come to a sampler tasting. "So you'll book your event with me!" Olivia had said. "And you can select your menu at the same time."

"That's great, Leen! Olivia's really good."

"I know. It'd be awesome, but I'm probably not qualified." Lena's eyes filled with the resigned look of expected rejection.

I gave her shoulders a quick squeeze. "Think positive. You never know."

After Lena was gone, my thoughts returned to my M&M's and Ho Hos, which, when I'd last seen them, had been brand new, intact in their packages. Maybe they still were.

It was amazing how a person's thoughts could turn on a dime. Now that I'd gotten rid of my treats, I wanted them back. Having proved I was a good girl, able to withstand my compulsive urges, it seemed like a shame to just throw all those tasty things away, particularly when they were calling to me.

It was wasteful, and I hated waste. In fact, it was downright irresponsible in a world where natural resources were disappearing and famine was on the rise.

They had to be in the ladies' room trash can, right? Where else could she have put them? I found myself skulking down the hallway to my destination, where I pretended to wash my hands while the receptionist in a neighboring suite refreshed her makeup and finally cleared the heck out.

"Bye!" I called to her. No sooner had the door swished shut than I plunged my hands into the trash, pushing aside paper towels and objects I didn't want to think about. I would have held my nose, but my hands were busy sorting through other people's filth.

Nothing. When I was shoulder-deep, I hit bottom. Hearing someone come in, I hastily pulled my hands out.

My food wasn't there. How, I didn't know, but my sister had outsmarted me.

As I slunk back to my office, I told myself to take it as a sign. Someone up there wanted me to get a clue.

Sixteen

Kaitlyn had been uncharacteristically silent recently, but now she was back at full throttle.

Less than two months to publication! Getting excited?

I've attached a copy of the book's cover. We're thrilled with it and are sure you will be too. It has just the right elegance, glamor, and romance needed to kick off this marketing campaign and your career as a writer with Fast Track. Soon I'll be sending a schedule of events and appearances for your day in New York— we plan to keep you very busy!

Kaitlyn

P.S. Can you believe that work can be so much fun?

No. I couldn't. I clicked on the attachment marked PASSION COVER. It blinked to life before my eyes.

Golden script reading *The Passion of Cecily*. An illustration of an exquisite woman with a cascade of auburn hair descending a stairway in a red evening gown. Its bodice was little more than a push-up corset that enclosed a minuscule waist and boobs displayed like two melons in a serving bowl. And, below the melons, the letters of my name.

Sabrina Hunter.

Me. My days, weeks, and years of hard work. My dreams coming true.

And yet . . . did Kaitlyn really expect me to look like my main character? Boy, was she gonna be disappointed. Why hadn't I warned her early on?

Oh, that's right. Because I was going to lose forty pounds. Silly me for forgetting.

This is the cover of my first book, I reminded myself. *Cherish this moment.* I would never have it again. And yet, because of my silly weight concerns, I was letting it be ruined.

And still, my brain continued to have fits. How did I plan to work parties in both New York and Los Angeles on the same night? How exactly had I gotten myself into that one again? I couldn't remember.

This wasn't like me. I was organized, responsible, good with details. I didn't create problems; I solved them. How had I turned the best thing that ever happened to me into such a mess?

I couldn't look at this cover anymore. I closed the email and logged off, done for the day. It was a strange week, what with Josh gone and hardly even bothering to call in. I'd asked him about Corinne, and he had responded with "She's fine," then asked about the menu for the *Circus Murders* party.

Thank God I was leaving early for our next scheduled softball game. The Monday night Gratitude Group and the Wednesday noon Conscious Eating Group were meeting for a historic showdown.

I had struggled with the clothing decision: Should I wear sweatpants that let me stoop and squat easily in my position as catcher, but made my ass look like a wobbling Jell-O mold? Or jeans, which held the jiggling ass in place, but didn't let me move? It was a tough choice. I wanted Daniel to desire me for my beauty *and* my talents. Even though he and I absolutely, positively weren't dating.

Then, genius struck. I would wear my new Firmfits under my sweatpants! Firmfits were undergarments that squeezed your fat into position. *To control and reshape*—that's what the advertisements said. I had just bought their capri-length leggings, which were perfect for today. I would play softball as gracefully as a gazelle, without a jiggle in sight.

"Hey, you!" Daniel caught up with me as I headed out onto the opposing team's softball field. He wore a gray T-shirt and faded jeans, and a lock of hair fell down into his eyes, all of it giving him an engaging guy-next-door quality. "You ready to catch some of my fastballs?"

"You bet!" I resisted the urge to yank at my Firmfits, which, due to gravity and downward pressure from my muffin top, were slowly descending. I would have to pull them up when he was looking in the other direction.

We stood around for a few minutes as people arrived. Michelle had gone conservative today in a navy-and-white track suit. She squeezed my arm and gave me a hug. "How's the program going for you?"

"Okay, although my sister did have to make an emergency visit." I told her how I'd enlisted Lena to throw away my sweets for me.

"Good for you." Michelle's eyes sparkled. "A few years ago, I'd have dived right into the trash after them!"

Inspired by her honesty, I found myself admitting, "Well, I did check out the ladies' room trash, but my stuff wasn't there."

Michelle laughed. "Sounds like your sister knows what she's doing. If you're really serious about throwing away food, you've gotta put it down the disposal. Or take it out of the package and mix it really well with, like, coffee grounds or something gross. If it's still in the package, it's like an open invitation to go get it."

"I suppose you could throw it into a dumpster," I said.

"No, it's too easy to climb into those dumpsters." Michelle waved her hand, dismissing my idea. "So remember, any time you want to binge, call me. Or anyone in the program. Just reach out."

"Thanks!" It was nice to realize all those doors were open to me, all those people were ready to listen and help if I needed it.

"Are you coming to the women's meeting next Tuesday night?" she asked.

"Yeah, I think so."

"Let's get started!" someone called. I felt a pleasant hum of anticipation. I hoped I'd have a chance to prove my batting skills.

I took my stance at home plate and raised my bat into the air. All my senses were on high alert for Daniel. On the mound across from me stood the other team's pitcher, Shirley R., a librarian with graying hair, eighteen years of mindful eating, and a determined gleam in her eye. "You're mine, Sabrina," she growled, rattling her charm bracelets as she wound up for the pitch.

I licked my lips and stared her down. "Bring it on, Shirley!" I wanted this. I wanted it bad. It was getting dark. The score was tied, with two outs.

"Go, Bree!" Michelle yelled from the sidelines. Daniel and my other teammates began to chant, "Bree, Bree, Bree!" It wasn't that they expected anything special from me, or had any reason to. It was just fun to cheer ourselves on.

Shirley unleashed a pitch that wobbled in my direction, sinking as it came. It hit the ground a foot in front of me and rolled.

"That all you got?" I yelled, swishing my hips.

"Just keeping you guessing!" Shirley fired back.

The second pitch, a much better one, flew at me. Carefully, my eye on the ball, I swung.

Thwack! The ball flew off my bat toward Shirley, who missed it, then bounced at Carla, the shortstop, who missed it, and continued in smaller and smaller bounces toward Ezra, the geriatric left outfielder.

Had Daniel seen that I'd gotten off a hit? I wanted to look around and check his reaction, but it wasn't a good time. I ran, rounding first base with my eye on Ezra, who ambled toward the ball, which lay on the ground. I would have had all the time in the world had my underwear stayed in place.

But no. Once again, my Firmfits began a slow journey downward, dragging my sweatpants with them. With the crotch of my pants inching downward, I had to shorten my stride, but I could still run.

What if my pants came off? Panicked, I grabbed my waistband and pulled as I half stepped it toward second.

"Bree, Bree, Bree!" my teammates screamed.

I passed second base, then looked back. Ezra had reached the ball and was fumbling to pick it up. Clutching my waistband, my breath tearing in my throat, I hobbled to third base while my team shouted, "Home run! Home run!" The Firmfits had crept even lower, pulling the crotch of my sweatpants to mid-thigh and forcing me into the tiny shuffling steps of an octogenarian. People were screaming, and I looked back again. Ezra got off a pretty good throw that headed straight for Shirley.

Determined to score, I minced on, my Firmfits—and the crotch of my pants—nearing my knees, hauling on the waistband of what had become the ultimate pair of high-rise sweatpants. Shirley hurled the ball, but it was too late. In teeny, tiny baby steps, I had crossed home plate.

"I did it!" I danced around, elated, surreptitiously trying to find Daniel. We'd won the game! I would have thrown both arms in the air, but I needed one to keep my pants up.

Shouting their approval, my teammates descended on me, yelling and pounding on my back. I returned hugs with one arm while the other continued to protect my decency. I readied myself to receive some hugging from Daniel, but he didn't materialize.

Mercifully, it was dark by then. Our huddle broke apart, allowing me to slink behind the corner of a building and wrestle my underwear into position. A bunch of people stood at a distance; they totally saw me do it, but at least they weren't people I knew. I waved to them, still glowing from my incredible success on the athletic field.

When I returned to my group, a lot of them had gone. I didn't see Daniel anywhere. Although I knew it was for the best, I drooped. Had he really left so soon, without saying a word to me?

Forget about him, I reminded myself. *He's seeing someone.*

The few people who remained were going to the Coffee Station, Michelle said. Did I want to go?

"I guess not," I told her. "I'm beat."

"Okay. See you tomorrow night at the meeting?"

"Yes!" I wished Daniel were still here.

Feeling let down, I headed for my car, then got an adrenaline rush when I saw a dark figure leaning against it. It was him. As he stepped into a pool of light, even I could see the warmth and admiration in his eyes.

I melted. "Hi."

He walked right up to me, grinning. "You really do it all, don't you? Write books, plan movie premieres, hit home runs?"

It was the second time he'd said something like that, but it still surprised me. I would never have thought my accomplishments would impress someone like him.

"You're an attorney. You fight for justice."

"Good thing," he said. "Otherwise, I'd have no shot at keeping up with you."

Was he flirting with me again? He'd been doing it the last time, at the Thai place, before that *Rachel* showed up. I couldn't help myself. I had to ask. "How's Rachel?"

He drew back the tiniest bit. "I haven't talked to her for a while."

"Oh?" I was a cool customer, all right. I said it like I couldn't care less.

He hesitated. "Okay, well. I guess I'll just . . . good night." He spoke slowly, as if this wasn't what he'd had in mind.

"Good night, Daniel." As I started my car, I wanted to kick myself. This wasn't what I'd had in mind, either.

What, then, did I have in mind? Spend time with Daniel, yes, but not if he was dating someone else.

I wanted to be the only girl in the picture, with any others long gone and forgotten. I wanted to walk on the beach with him, sip a glass of wine, hold hands, tell him things I'd never told anyone else. Maybe I wanted to be in love with him, although love seemed overrated to me, just something destined to disappoint.

Despite my speeding as I drove away from the softball field, I still wasn't going fast enough to escape my whirling thoughts about the people I'd loved, who had all abandoned me in one way or another.

I never really grieved when Mom left and Dad withdrew into his own world—I didn't have time. At age nine, I'd had to make sure my little sister ate and got to school and went to bed on time. I had to explain things to her, even if I myself didn't know the answers to her questions.

Why did Mama leave us? Why doesn't Daddy love us anymore?

I didn't know.

Similarly, I didn't grieve openly when Mark moved out. I was busy, with finals coming up along with a move back to California. *It's all good,* I told people. *I guess it just ran its course.*

I was civil and didn't cry or beg. I let him keep both the waterbed and the coffeemaker.

But I'd never forgotten or forgiven. I hadn't spoken to either Mom or Mark in years, and even Dad, I avoided. We'd exchanged voicemails at Christmas but hadn't talked since last year sometime.

More memories came back to me. Christmases when our family was happily all together. Mark and I vacationing in Nantucket, just the two of us, when we were so in love.

A craving crept over me like a wave of poisoned gas. A craving for nachos—that explosion of flavors and textures—cheesy, greasy, salty, chewy, and crunchy all at the same time. They were the most delicious things in the world. Of course, I just happened to know the location of the nearest TacoLand drive-through.

However, just because I made the left turn toward TacoLand didn't mean that I was actually going to go there. It didn't mean I was actually going to buy nachos and eat them. And just because I made the next turn on the route toward TacoLand didn't mean that I was going to binge and destroy the small amount of progress that I'd made. I was just going to drive by the place and have a look.

But once I'd had a look, it seemed a pity not to stop for a little something, just for old time's sake. Like a double order of nachos and a jumbo orange soda.

I exited the TacoLand parking lot, drove a few blocks, and pulled over. There, sitting in the front seat of my car, I inhaled the nachos, which were soggy and oversalted. They were nothing like my fantasy of them, but that didn't stop me from consuming the whole giant boxful.

The second I had finished, I was sorry. I couldn't believe I'd done that. I couldn't believe I was allowed to exist. There was no hope for me. I was ugly. I was fat. I was a total failure.

How was I a loser? I would count the ways. I was screwing up my first book launch after waiting for it all my life. I was screwing up the program by my incessant cheating. And to top it off, Daniel would sooner or later see me for what I was and then for sure he would absolutely, positively never date me or love me.

Seventeen

The next morning, I smacked the ringing alarm clock harder than necessary, then put a hand over my mouth to check out my nacho breath. It was bad. Thank goodness I always set my alarm early, allowing myself an extra fifteen minutes in bed.

I burped as I turned over. I would have to pop antacids for breakfast. Then, after I felt better, I'd hit McDonald's for a double egg McMuffin chaser.

I stopped myself. I had to meet with Michelle tomorrow. How many sins did I want to confess to, after all? The Nacho Incident was bad enough.

Of course, I didn't have to tell her any of it. It was just that, for some reason, lying didn't come as easily as it used to.

On impulse, I grabbed my cell from the bedside table and called Lena. "Wake up!" I yelled into the phone upon hearing her muffled, sleepy "Hello?"

In the background, I heard movement and Stuart's voice, which was considerably more alert than Lena's.

"It's Bree," Lena mumbled to Stuart. "You talk to her. You're awake."

The next thing I knew, he was on the line. "Hey, Bree, thanks for the Ho Hos! And the M&M's too!"

I sucked in my breath. *Lena and Stuart ate my Ho Hos?*

Stuart kept talking. "Any time you wanna get rid of food, give us a call!"

It was so not fair that they got to eat my stuff when I couldn't.

"I asked her to throw that stuff away!"

"Why? It was awesome!"

Focus, I told myself. I forced myself to get down to the burning issue at hand. "Stuart, I had nachos last night. I don't want to do it again."

"Then don't."

"But it's not that easy!"

"It's not easy, but it's simple." Stuart's voice held a note of quiet conviction.

"What's that supposed to mean?"

"For me, it means I do what my sponsor tells me."

"You just blindly obey?"

"Might as well. It's not like my way of doing things was working for me."

True. I could say the same.

Lena's voice sounded in the background, then Stuart spoke again. "She says to tell you she can't make the catering thing next week. She's got a doctor's appointment."

I had invited Lena to come with me to Olivia's tasting reception. It would help me choose the party menu and, just as important, provide a free lunch.

This was bad news. "Crap. I don't want to go alone!"

"Sorry." He sounded like he meant it. "I gotta take off. I got three surfing lessons to teach." A pause. "You gonna be okay?"

"Yeah," I moaned. But I wasn't sure.

"See you Saturday at the beach? Lesson number two?"

"Yes!" It cheered me up to think of tackling those waves again.

Talking to Stuart had rebalanced me. I went to work with my turkey sandwich, carrot sticks, and an apple. One day at a time. *I will start fresh today,* I thought as I sat down at my computer and opened my email.

I groaned when I saw the message from Kaitlyn.

> *I'm passing along the reminder from marketing to bring two different outfits (slacks and a blazer or a suitable dress) for the day events. Of course, don't forget that all-important evening gown for the party!*

Of course. One mustn't forget one's evening gown. I would have to buy shoes too, I supposed, a pair of glittery, ankle-breaking stilettos that I would never wear again. What, no tiara? Maybe Kaitlyn could loan me one of hers.

Tie me to an anchor. Send me down to the other bottom-feeders.

In the midst of my dark thoughts, the phone rang.

It was Josh. I really wanted to know how he and Corinne were doing. "Hey, how's Corinne?" I asked.

His voice seemed to come from a great distance. "She's going to be at a hospital here in Houston for the next six weeks. These guys are supposed to be the best, but I don't know. I'm gonna stick around, keep an eye on 'em."

"Where will you stay?" My mind ran through the implications of what he'd just said.

"Hotel down the street." Josh rushed on, apparently unconcerned by details like his own comfort. "You gotta help me, Sabrina. I need you to man the office for a while."

"Really? Are you sure?" I couldn't believe he'd give me that much responsibility.

"I'm serious." A note of desperation underlaid his voice. "I'll call in every day to go over what we should do."

"What do you want me to tell the clients about your absence?"

"When they call, tell them I'm unavailable and will be back in six weeks."

"Wouldn't it be a lot more efficient to send out a letter explaining what's happening? That way, we inform everybody all at once and also nip any rumors in the bud before they spread."

Josh was silent as he considered my suggestion. A second later, "Draft up the letter for me to review." A pause. "Good idea."

Victory! Compliments from Josh came around about as often as Halley's Comet. "Thank you. Shall I just say that your wife's become ill and you've gone with her to Texas to seek treatment? And that you'll stay in close touch and will be back in six weeks?"

"Okay." He peppered me with instructions about things I'd already anticipated and handled, then hung up.

My brain was charging along, sorting through all the stuff I had to do, both personal and work-related. I'd have no choice but to buy all new clothes for my trip to New York. Virtually nothing in my closet was good enough. Of course, I would wait until the very last minute, just in case those forty pounds decided to drop off by themselves. The thought of trying to find half a dozen outfits that would make me look chic and elegant at my current weight sent me into a fit of clammy sweats.

I also had to go to three program meetings a week, call and meet regularly with Michelle, and plan and track my food. Softball and surfing—well, I supposed I didn't have to do them, but I wanted to. They were for my sanity.

As for the party, I had to choose the menu, attend to a million last-minute details, and figure out how to supervise it at a distance of three thousand miles—without screwing it up.

And now I had to turn into Josh's mini-me. In some ways, it would be easier with him two thousand miles away. I wouldn't have to hear his angry outbursts or run his personal errands. I could work faster without him around interrupting, changing his mind, and losing things. And how awesome was this? I could patch phones through to my cell and work from home.

Or from my fitting room at the mall.

I brightened. This new arrangement might have possibilities, after all.

And last on my list of things to do: make Daniel fall madly and permanently in love with me. Not something I had to do, but I wanted to. Too bad it was the only thing I had absolutely, positively no idea how to accomplish.

"You ready to try the pop-up?" Stuart asked. We stood with our boards at the ocean's edge, preparing to paddle out. The waves were, if anything, bigger than they were last week, the water a dark blue in the sunlight.

From a towel nearby, Lena waved her sunscreen bottle. "Have fun, kids!" My sister had begged off surfing in favor of sun worship. She tossed back her hair and stretched out on the towel, sizzling in an almost-not-there red bikini. Next to her, in my wet suit, I looked like a gargantuan rubber bathtub toy.

For the millionth time, I contemplated the fact that she and I came from the same gene pool. But no, I wasn't bitter. I would hold no grudges. I would rise above the fact that I was clearly shorted when the DNA got handed out.

"Ready," I said to Stuart. My head was full of instructions. Lie on the center of the board, keep my hands under my chest and my legs together on the board, push with hands and toes, and spring to my feet. All while a giant wave was propelling me along at a death-defying speed.

Sure, I could do that. Maybe. My whole body thrummed with anticipation.

"All right, first we travel out beyond the breaking waves." We paddled hard with our arms, passing over a couple of waves, and bringing ourselves into position. I was glad my body seemed to remember what to do from the last time.

"In the beginning, I'm just going to tell you when to paddle and when to pop up, okay? Later, you'll start to read the waves on your own." Stuart was looking over his shoulder. "Okay, it's coming . . . now go!"

I paddled, my arms windmilling, as the wave pushed us along. Beside me, Stuart made long, forceful strokes through the water, looking over his shoulder. My board rose as the wave brought us up with the ease of a giant blowing dandelion seeds.

"Pop up *now!*"

I pushed with my hands and toes. For a split second, my feet found the board, which tipped sideways, tumbling me into the wave. Bowled over, it took me a second to get my bearings, but then I shot up past the surface, gulping air.

Stuart was beside me, straddling his board. "You weren't centered."

"Okay." Spitting water, I paddled out again with Stuart next to me. Together, we waited.

"Okay, paddle . . . *pop up!*"

Instantly, I fell again.

"You were late."

I tried it again. And again. And again. Each time, Stuart told me what I needed to do differently. Hands centered under my chest and not out on the rails. Come to standing in a single smooth motion. Feet centered on the board. Stand facing sideways, not forward.

My hair streamed water, my eyes burned from the salt, my nose was running snot down my chin. I could feel bruises starting on my calves and thighs.

I loved it.

"You want to call it a day?" Stuart asked, taking pity on me.

"No way! I got this!" The water was cool and buoyant, and it sparkled in the sunshine. I was going to do this—I could feel it. "I'm gonna own this next wave."

"Okay, get set . . . paddle!"

My arms sliced through the water, propelling me forward even as I felt the wave coming up behind me, lifting the tail of my board. It was time to go. As Stuart yelled "Pop up!" I was already pushing with my fingers and toes, feeling my feet hit the board just right, the incredible force of the ocean lifting me up and forward as I stood, my board skimming along just before the curve of the wave. I raised my arms over my head, elated.

One coherent thought crossed my mind: *I'm standing in the hand of God.*

And then I fell.

Stuart was there, reaching out to me when I bobbed to the surface. "Awesome!" he yelled. "Do you know how hard that is to do?" His teeth gleamed a brilliant white against his tan. "You wanna try again?"

"Yes!"

A dozen more times I paddled out and rode a wave in, or tried to. On my last one, I stayed up for a minute or more, riding almost all the way into shore. Lena stood on the beach, applauding, while Stuart helped me get my board and walk in through the surf.

"She's a natural!" he said to Lena.

"Bree, you were so great!" Lena said. "I couldn't pop up for ages, and I never got very good at it."

"Yeah, but no one was ever more beautiful trying," Stuart said.

"Aw, honey." She curved her hand around his neck and drew him closer, clearly unconcerned about the salt water dripping off him. "You're sweet."

"Not as sweet as you."

In a minute, they'd be making out, or worse. I grabbed a towel and dried off my hair, then peeled off my wet suit, not caring anymore who might see me in my black one-piece swimsuit. My whole body glowed from the exertion and from the thrill of standing on that board, slicing through the water, using all that power and force beneath me to carry me along. It was an otherworldly experience.

We began the trudge back to the parking lot, carrying our boards and towels, our feet sinking deeply into the sand with every step, my tired muscles once again working hard. It felt good.

"So next Saturday, Bree?" Stuart said. "We can make it a regular lesson for you."

"I'd love to, but . . . you should spend your time on paying customers, not me."

He waved it off. "I want to do it." He paused, as if making a pronouncement, then said, "After all, you're family." We had reached the edge of the parking lot and stopped to put on flip-flops to protect our feet from the hot, rough asphalt.

It took a second for Stuart's statement to sink in. He and Lena had drawn together, beaming and looking at me expectantly. When I continued to draw a blank, Lena raised her left hand and made a production of coughing into it.

That's when I saw the ring. She for sure hadn't been wearing it earlier while she rubbed sunscreen into her arms. She'd been brave, or foolish, to bring it to a public beach where it could disappear as easily as a feather in a hurricane.

"Oh, Lena!" I looked in awe at the sparkling object on her hand. A large round diamond rested within a circle of smaller diamonds. Just to be sure there were enough diamonds on the thing, the band around her finger was also set with a row of another twenty or so small ones. Graceful and delicate, the ring sat on Lena's finger like a little miracle, the most beautiful piece of jewelry I'd ever seen.

I suddenly remembered that Stuart had only recently been able to pay me back the last of the hundred dollars I'd loaned him. How had he bought this ring on a surf instructor's wages?

"It was my Aunt Veronica's," Stuart said. "When she died, my mama got the ring. Mama always said it would go to the first one of us boys who got engaged."

He and Lena both looked at it as if they couldn't quite believe it was theirs. But of course it was. Stuart was just playing at being poor. He would come into his trust fund in a few more years, and Lena along with him.

"When did this happen? Where? Tell me everything!" I hugged Lena, so happy for her, yet thinking *four years younger*. My screw-up baby sister was getting married ahead of me, and to a gorgeous, wealthy guy who worshiped her. I should get so lucky.

"We haven't decided," Lena said. "I've always wanted a big, traditional wedding, but . . ." She sighed. "I don't know who would pay for it."

I tried not to look at Stuart, but he got my drift anyway.

"We were lucky Mom gave us the ring," he told me. "And that they haven't disinherited me."

"They would do that?"

"Membership in the Livingston family comes with strings." Stuart adopted a light tone. "They weren't happy when I refused to become a sheet designer."

Lena gazed at me beseechingly. "Do you think . . . Dad would chip in?"

"Oh, honey . . ." I had longed ago stopped expecting anything from our father.

"I still say we elope," Stuart said, finally beginning to pull off his wet suit and towel.

"Even if they won't pay for the wedding, we have to consider your parents' feelings," Lena said. "I want them to like me."

"Who could ever not like you?" Again, Stuart spoke in a light tone, but I saw his troubled expression.

"You'd be surprised." Lena's eyes cut to me. We could both remember several sets of parents who had blamed the irrepressible Lena of earlier days for their sons' skirmishes with drugs, wild parties, and the police. "It's important to me, Stuart."

"I know, baby," he said. "It's just, I stopped trying to please my parents a long time ago."

"The other thing is"—she was talking to me now—"I want Dad to give me away." She looked at me sideways, waiting for my response.

This was really bad. "We don't even know where he is anymore!"

"I tracked him down through his job, and I'm gonna call him." Lena said it in her please-don't-be-mad voice.

That struck me like a bolt of lightning. "Well, don't expect me to even be in the same room with him!" After everything he'd done, I couldn't understand why Lena still reached out to him or cared what he thought. "He doesn't love us."

"I think he does," she said quietly.

"Omigod!"

"Bree, if I find him, will you be nice to him?"

"Honestly? I don't know if I can."

"*Please?*"

Guilt whispered in my ear. I shouldn't spoil Lena's big day—I should say yes. But I couldn't. "Anything else you want?" I grumbled.

"Be my maid of honor."

"That I can do." I was still cranky. "So long as I don't have to wear a sleeveless dress."

"Fine."

"Or one of those empire waists that cuts me across the middle and makes me look like a fire hydrant."

"Fine."

"No tea-length, either."

"Bree! You don't have to wear anything you don't want to."

"Okay then." More guilt. Lena deserved my support. I waded over to her in the sand and folded my arms around her. "I'm really glad for you, baby sister."

She kissed me on the cheek. "Thanks. That means a lot."

"I love you," I said. *Just don't make me talk to Dad.*

Eighteen

I dragged a heavy backpack behind me up a flight of wooden stairs, its wheels bumping on every step. Inside was program literature available for members to purchase at cost—*A Guide to the Twelve Steps*, daily readers offering inspirational thoughts, pamphlets on mindful eating. I had kept my promise to Michelle to take a program job. As the group's so-called publications person, it would be my job for the next six months to keep the backpack filled and bring it to this Thursday night meeting every week. Assuming I lasted that long.

It was all part of being of service, which was the program's holy grail. You sought to be of service to your friends, your community, to humanity in general. It was commendable, I admitted grudgingly to myself, but I still didn't see what it had to do with my fitting into that red dress.

"Hi, Sabrina!" The group's current greeter hailed me at the door. Last week, when the semiannual job swap had occurred, I had eyed the greeter job, pegging it as cushy until I realized it required you to arrive fifteen minutes early. Heck no, that wasn't going to happen.

"Hi!" How embarrassing. They all knew my name, and I couldn't remember theirs.

As I slipped into the room, the first person I saw was Daniel. Very conveniently, he just happened to attend this meeting regularly, making it easier for me to stalk him.

He caught my eye and waved me over. What a relief that we seemed to have put behind us that ghastly awkwardness over Rachel. I'd finally convinced myself that she didn't matter to me anymore. Of course he'd been dating women before he met me; there was nothing wrong with that. And now that he'd met me, I just had to convince him that I was the one for him. Easy, right?

"No one's sitting here." He pulled his jacket off the seat next to him, offering it to me, while a couple of nearby women gave me the stink eye. He was freshly shaved and smelled of lemon.

Trying to breathe him in inconspicuously, I sat down, wondering if he had saved the chair specifically for me. Even if he had, it might not mean anything; maybe it was just his way of continuing to welcome me in as a still newish member of the group.

The meeting started. As usual, we said the Serenity Prayer, and for the first time, I really listened to the words. *God, grant me the serenity to accept the things I cannot change . . .* That made sense. No point in hitting your head against a brick wall. *The courage to change the things I can . . .* Again, I couldn't argue with that. *And the wisdom to know the difference.*

Did I have the wisdom to know the difference? What were the things in my life that I could change? What were the things I would never have, the things I had to stop hoping for? A thick lump formed in my throat. Maybe I would never be a successful author. Fast Track would change its mind about me when they learned the truth. If they couldn't cancel my contract expressly because of my weight, they might look for other reasons to wiggle out of it. They might drop me down to second or third priority for marketing or editorial dollars.

Or maybe my books simply wouldn't be good enough. People would never read and love my stories the way I'd dreamed.

For that matter, maybe I would always be fat. Maybe I should give up on ever being slender and pretty and just accept myself the way I was right now. Is that what the prayer was telling me?

This week's leader began to speak. "I'm Rose, and I'm a compulsive overeater-slash-bulimic—and a sugar addict." She wore a dark green sweater and jeans and twirled a piece of auburn hair around her finger. "Twelve years ago, I lost one hundred fifty pounds through the program and kept it off for six years. But then"—she shook her head as if to clear it—"the disease came back. I started snacking and then bingeing. I gained back eighty pounds. For three more years, I floundered through every diet, fast, program, and fix I could find—except the one that I knew would help me."

I couldn't believe it. To have lost so much weight and kept if off, only to throw away all that success!

Rose continued: "You've got to do the work—every day! It's super hard, but at least these rooms are always there for me. I'm so thankful for that."

It was true. In the program, the people were always kind and on your side. Always willing to give you a minute of their time.

I had to admit, it was nice to know a place that was totally, completely safe.

The meeting closed as usual, as the group joined hands in a circle for the final prayer. Daniel took mine while I repressed a moan of ecstasy. As his hand tightened around mine, the prayer ended all too soon. Was it my imagination, or did he hold my hand a second longer than he had to?

"So, Sabrina!" Daniel said in my ear as we filtered out of the room afterward. He glanced over at me maneuvering my wheeled literature backpack toward the stairs. "I'll take that." He swung it up by the handle and carried it down the stairs while I trotted beside him.

"How'd you like the meeting?" he asked.

"I was thinking about the Serenity Prayer," I told him. "I mean, how are you supposed to know what you should keep trying for in your life and what you should give up on?"

Daniel cocked his head at me. "You mean, how do you know what things you can and cannot change?"

"Yeah. Like, what if I never make it as a writer? I have no control over that."

We reached the end of the hallway and burst through the door into the cool evening air. At eight o'clock, the summer sky was still light.

Daniel stopped walking and turned to face me. I found myself looking up at him, but then, at five-foot-one, I looked up to just about everybody. Daniel was probably five-foot-nine—not tall enough for some women, but perfect for me. I could wear any heels I wanted with him, yet even barefoot, I wouldn't have to crank my head back at a painful angle to kiss him. Which hadn't happened, but a girl could always hope. I couldn't help but notice a few program members eyeing the fact that I had Daniel's attention.

He was answering my question. "The way I read the Serenity Prayer, the only thing you can change is yourself—your thoughts, your words, your behavior. What you can't change is everything and everybody else."

"So, becoming a best-selling writer . . . ?"

"Is out of your control, except for the hard work you put into it."

I nodded, although my mind rebelled. "I want to make it happen!"

He laughed. "Don't we all?" We stood, smiling at each other for a minute. Then, "You doing anything special this weekend?"

Why was he asking? "Saturday afternoon, I'm going to a tasting reception put on by this caterer I'm using for the *Circus Murders* party." My heart started to pound as an idea came to me. "I asked my sister to come, but she can't make it."

"Too bad," he said. He glanced over at me as we began walking again to our cars.

My heart pounded even harder. "Um. Would you like to come along?" The words came out almost too softly to hear them. "The food should be good," I added helpfully.

"Sure, why not?" His eyes, electric blue pools with flecks of green, stared into mine with . . . I tried to identify the emotion there. Interest? Admiration?

Regardless, he'd said yes!

"We can meet there," I said.

"How about I pick you up? If it's okay with you?"

The look in his eyes was definitely interest. This was a date for sure, right? If he picked me up and drove, that would count as a date, wouldn't it?

It didn't matter. I would see him on Saturday. Oh, God, what would I wear?

I usually bought clothes online, but with one day to find an outfit for Saturday's date, I was forced to hit the stores for the first time in years. I told myself that I had to start looking anyway for New York, so this would be good practice. Or, if I got lucky, I'd be able to use my date dress in New York as well.

I had recruited expert help. During my lunch hour on Friday, Lena led me, hyperventilating, through the crowded cosmetics section of one of LA's posh and enormous department stores. As I ducked past a trio of girls testing blush, a saleswoman tried to squirt me with perfume. I dodged her just in time.

"Women's clothes are on the second floor," Lena announced. "Follow me!"

That made sense. The department stores devoted less than a quarter of their first floors to men's clothing, but their entire second floors to women's. I supposed this was due to women's assumed predilection for shopping, combined with the acute importance that appearance was felt to play in our identities.

"We have to find the plus-size department," I whispered to Lena. It would be our surest bet for finding something quickly on what was turning out to be a busy day at the office. I was patching all calls through to my cell, answering only the ones that couldn't wait and sending the rest to voicemail. I was not going home today without something to wear. I could feel myself start to hyperventilate, a rash sprouting on my knees and elbows.

"Here's a store directory," Lena said. "What would it be called?"

We looked at the departments listed under women's clothing. Point of View. Trending. Equilibrium. Unlimited.

"I don't know a lot of these," Lena said, her brow crinkling.

"Why don't they just say *Fat Clothes*?" I demanded.

"This is useless," Lena said. "Let's go upstairs and ask someone."

We took the escalator. As we ascended from the jewelry and handbag counters, where my buying status was equal to anyone's, into the realm of women's fashion, I felt myself becoming more and more transparent until I was almost invisible, someone that salespeople looked right through without seeing. If you couldn't fit into the clothes they sold, you were of no interest to them.

We arrived at the top to a full panorama of spring and summer clothes. Mannequins stood swathed in soft, cool fabrics like cotton and linen. To my left were rows of clothes in creamy pastels, while ahead I saw white enlivened by bright splashes of color—peach and a ruby red and a lime green. Trendy music thumped in the background.

I shrank into myself a little, thinking, *Be brave!*

Women buzzed around the clothing racks like flies on meat. It amazed me that so many women were free to shop in the middle of a workday. Even if it was a Friday. Maybe they'd taken three-day weekends, but I doubted it.

Lena had found a salesperson. "Where are the plus-size clothes?" she asked.

"Honey, you don't need that." The woman's name tag said LAWANDA. She had a head full of tiny braids, an armful of bracelets, and a leopard-patterned dress.

"No, it's for . . ." Lena stopped, but LaWanda had already spotted me.

"Oh, I see. Third floor. Look for The Stately Woman."

"But all the women's clothes are on two," Lena protested.

"What you're looking for's on three."

I obediently followed Lena up another escalator. It was all coming back to me—the indignity of shopping for the overweight and why I stopped going to clothing stores. A glumness settled over me.

As we reached the third floor, the music had stopped. No sound of voices anywhere. We walked past a display of luggage, our footsteps echoing. As we entered housewares, a frown crept onto Lena's face.

A salesman, the first person we'd seen, hurried in our direction. "Rice cookers are on clearance," he announced, his face hopeful.

Lena frowned some more. "Where's The Stately Woman?" she barked.

He pointed. "Past the vacuum cleaners."

We finally found our destination in a distant corner of the store. No mannequins, no glitzy displays. A selection of jackets and dresses drooped from hangers. There was not a salesperson in sight.

Lena let out a long breath. I could almost see her mentally rallying. "*Okay*! Let's get to work."

"I guess pulling this over my head wasn't such a good idea." I crumpled onto the little bench in our fitting room, a tangerine-colored dress tangled into a viselike grip around my shoulders and boobs. As this point, my arms trapped over my head in the tight fabric, I couldn't get the dress to move either up or down.

"I got it," Lena said, carefully working the hateful garment up and off me.

I'd tried a dozen outfits, each more dreadful than the last. "This is impossible!"

She skewered me with a glare. "The problem isn't you. It's the clothes. Always remember that."

What would she know about it? She stood there in a little sleeveless, backless sundress, her legs looking long and slender beneath the skirt that ended mid-thigh. It was probably a size six or eight. Her hair, normally brown, was turning sun-streaked like Stuart's. Then there was that glow of happiness, or maybe it was just the glow from the rock on her hand. She looked as good as I'd ever seen her.

Squinting her eyes in concentration, she sorted through the clothes we'd brought in while I wallowed in self-pity on my bench. "I'm going to try again. Wait here," she said to me and marched out. Ten minutes went by until the curtain flew open again. She was back with another armful of clothes, which she set on the bench and pointed to meaningfully. Sighing, I picked up the first item, a flowered skirt, and got back to work.

At the exact moment that we found the perfect outfit, Alexa Fredericks called to say she loved the script I'd sent.

"You did? That's great!" I said into my cell phone as Lena zipped me into the prettiest summer dress I'd ever seen. It was about the twentieth thing I'd tried, but it was worth the effort. Its soft lilac brought color to my cheeks and brightened my eyes, which were usually a washed-out gray-blue.

"Omigod! It's incredible!" Lena mouthed to me.

I stared at myself. The V-neck that dipped down toward a narrowed waist, the skirt that suddenly swirled out, the little flutter of a cap sleeve—it all slimmed and flattered in a way that I couldn't believe would be possible on my body.

On the phone, Alexa was going on. "Is Josh there? He's got to get me the rights to this script!"

Lena was surveying every inch of me with the excitement of a proud mother. Hem length, check. Sleeves, check. Even I had to admit, I looked good in this dress. Not tiny, or even thin, but still . . . curvy and pretty. It was a revelation. I stared into the mirror while I spoke.

"Josh is still away on personal business, but I speak to him daily. I'll make sure he calls you later today." While Lena fussed with my skirt, I gave Alexa my cell number so she could reach me anytime—maybe not the wisest move, but I wanted to get this client.

"Is it too dressy?" I asked Lena the instant I hung up the phone.

"No way! It's the perfect little day dress. It'll knock his socks off!" Lena looked as if she would burst with pride. "And who picked this one out, by the way?"

"You, darling sister. I give you all the credit."

"This style is so good on you. Let's remember it when we choose your maid of honor dress." Lena pulled out her iPhone and took a couple of snapshots.

It blew me away to think that I could go on a date tomorrow with Daniel and feel self-confident. "Do you think I could wear this in New York? Like for a book signing?"

"You bet! And we can find more stuff too. We'll go out again in a few weeks."

"Thanks, Leen." For the first time since Kaitlyn's marketing memo, a wisp of hope arose. Maybe I could get through this, after all.

I got back to the office by 3:30 and called Josh. "Alexa Fredericks loves *Dead by Midnight*. We got her! She's going to sign!" Exhilarated, seated in my office chair, I spun myself in a full circle.

Low voices in the background and the rustle of movement. "I can get more for the script if I negotiate it separately from the client contract. Sorry, would you hold for a minute?" Josh sounded flat and dead, as if he'd aged ten years.

A minute or two went by, while I waited, impatiently tapping my foot.

"Sabrina? Yeah . . . sorry," Josh said again. "Things are bad here, and I'm in a meeting right now with Corinne's doctors."

"Alexa Fredericks wants to sign with us!"

"Hold on." He disappeared again, then came back. "Shit! Alexa wants to sign *now?*" If a voice could stagger and fall, that's what Josh's did. "Corinne's a lot worse."

"I'm so sorry. Are . . . are the doctors recommending a treatment plan?"

"Yeah, but she's still having psychotic episodes. She thinks the Lawn People have followed her to Texas. Yesterday, she barricaded herself in her room, and they had to remove the fucking door to get her out."

Josh had never sounded so low, so discouraged. I swallowed hard, trying to think of a reply. How could I help him?

I'd learned a lot watching Josh over the last three years. "Listen," I said. "I'll get Alexa to sign the contract. You just take care of Corinne."

He was talking to someone in the room with him. I wasn't sure he'd heard me until he said, "Okay. I gotta go. Tell Alexa I'll call her as soon as I can."

"Yep." I was glad he couldn't see me quaking like a leaf. What was I thinking? I wasn't an agent. I would mess up. He must be out of his mind with worry about Corinne to leave so much responsibility to me.

My computer beeped: an email from Kaitlyn. I groaned. Now what did she want?

Hello, Sabrina!

I've attached forty separate interview questions for you to answer in writing.

Forty interview questions? There weren't forty things about me worth discussing. I wasn't that interesting.

They've been compiled from interviews that will run in twenty different blogs in the first month of publication. Even though some of the questions ask pretty much the same things, please try to give a different spin to each answer. We don't want to give our audience the same stock answers in every blog they read.

So I was supposed to come up with forty different ways to say the same thing.

Nothing but fun and games here!

We've gotten some really great early reviews, which I've attached! We continue to be so excited about your book and your fabulous launch!

Thrilled, I tore into the reviews. Heck yeah! For good reviews, I could come up with forty ways to say the same thing. I'd wanted this more than anything, and now, maybe, just maybe, it was coming through. I called Alexa back.

"Hi there! Sabrina again." I explained that Josh was attending to his dangerously ill wife, but that he was thrilled to be representing her and wanted to sign her immediately. "Josh will be in touch with you as soon as he can, but in the meantime, I can help you get started and orient you to our agency."

Alexa clicked her tongue in disapproval. "Josh promised me his full personal attention. He said that was the main reason to go to a small agency like his."

"You'll have Josh's full attention," I promised. "It's just that, his wife is actually in a very serious health crisis right now. He has to be with her."

"I guess." Alexa didn't sound sure about that.

"He'll be back soon. And in the meantime, I have a fresh copy of the contract all ready for you!" I said it all perky and excited, as if nothing could be more wonderful. "Shall I bring it over to you? Josh prefers to send hard copies to his clients."

"Messenger it to my business manager. And talk to Josh about getting me that script!" She hung up.

I sat holding the dead phone. Another heartwarming moment in the life of a Hollywood executive assistant. Fortunately, one of the things I'd learned in my years here was how to suck up.

I placed a call to Josh's preferred florist. "I need a dozen super-fresh pink peonies in a crystal vase. The message on the card should read, *To my number one client. Great things are ahead! Best, Josh.*" I gave Alexa's address and put a rush on it: "I need it delivered today, please."

I then placed a rush order for a dozen giant Mylar balloons with sayings like CONGRATULATIONS! and YOU'RE THE BEST! and sent them to Alexa with another card:

> *Here's my cell phone number again. Call me anytime you need something—promise? I'm thrilled to be working with you!*
>
> —*Sabrina*

Finally, I arranged for a messenger to take her another copy of the contract. "Please deliver this today."

I crossed my fingers and prayed my little offerings would satisfy Alexa's need to be the center of the universe and give Josh some time to resolve the Corinne situation and come home. If I had to, I would personally go pick up the signed contract myself.

I had to say, I was pretty good at getting things done . . . as long as it didn't involve my own life. Yet I still had so much to do. My brain buzzed with all of it. *Come on, Sabrina. Think. Prioritize. Make lists.*

I couldn't. I was tired. I would go home and take a bath.

In my apartment, I lit candles and poured myself an inch of wine. I set my laptop on the bathroom counter and found some online spa music—harp with a smattering of flute. I poured in bath salts and let them dissolve.

What a great idea—a nice, soothing bath. The first notes of music sounded as I slid down into the warm, lavender-scented water. I sighed.

This was so delicious.

It was then I realized that no matter how stressed out or discouraged I'd been today, it had not once occurred to me to binge.

Nineteen

Wearing my spectacular new summer dress, I opened the door for Daniel.

All he said was, "You look good."

But it was the way he said it, in this carefully casual yet really intense way. It was right up there with "My name is Bond. James Bond." Manly, no words wasted. Sexy.

He proceeded to walk me down the front stairs of my building to his car, the cool-because-it's-ecologically-sensitive hybrid I expected him to have, then opened the door for me and took my hand to help me inside.

"Thanks." My eyes met his with what I could only call a soul-jolt. Did he feel it too?

Still playing the gentleman, he ran around the back of his car and jumped in the driver's side, folding his legs in under the dashboard. "So where to?" he asked, giving me that look again. Any defenses I might have put up to protect myself from heartbreak were crumbling under the onslaught of this chemistry we felt. Or at least, I felt it, for him.

Daniel, I'd come to realize, was the master of eye contact. He made eye contact the way Dolly Parton wrote a song, or John Grisham a book. He was a natural, and he did it a lot. There, he was doing it right now. One soulful glance, and I was obliterated.

I smoothed my hands along my skirt as we drove to Olivia's, a tea and sandwich shop that also served as the base of Olivia's catering business. As we walked up, people waited outside the entrance. The place was closed but would open in a couple of minutes for our private event.

"I forgot to feed the meter," Daniel said. "Be right back!" He jogged off, leaving me standing alone. I watched him go, thinking he looked good from this direction too.

Behind me, a male voice. "That you, Bree?"

I spun around. "Stuart? What are you doing here?"

His hair in a neat bun at the base of his neck, he wore a Hawaiian shirt, cotton pants, and flip-flops. A leather braid ran around one wrist. "Lena sent me."

I stared at him. "She did? Why?"

"She sent me in her place. So you don't have to do this thing alone." Stuart's eyebrows knitted together as he spoke.

"I'm not alone!" My eyes swept down the street, searching for Daniel. Here, Stuart was being so thoughtful, yet all I wanted was to get rid of him. For this first date with Daniel, I hadn't envisioned bringing along a sidekick.

Stuart was giving me a once-over. "Is this the dress Lena helped you buy?"

"The very one."

"I thought you were gonna wear it tonight, for your big date."

"No, my big date's not—"

"We've got two hours of parking now." Daniel loomed up beside me, a quizzical expression on his face as he glanced back and forth between Stuart and me.

"Anyway," Stuart went on, oblivious, "it's awesome. Dude, you're hot!"

I had tried to cut him off, but not quickly enough. "Stuart, this is my friend Daniel. Daniel, this is Stuart. I didn't know he was coming!"

"Hey, man." Stuart stuck out his hand, friendly as a puppy. "Isn't this great? Free food!"

"I know. You gotta love it!" I said, while inwardly, I heaved a sigh.

Stuart was taller and leaner and sported a tanned, sun-streaked surfer look, while Daniel was more the muscular, classically hand-some all-American guy. On the bright side of things, they were two smoking hot men. And they were both with me. I preened a little for the girls who eyed us as they passed by in the street.

Stuart turned toward me. "How do you guys know each other?"

I couldn't give a direct answer to Stuart's question. It would breach Daniel's privacy to say we'd met in the program, and all I cared about anyway was making sure Daniel knew who Stuart was to me. I gave my answer straight to Daniel. "This is my sister's fiancé. And he's my surfing instructor too."

Daniel perked up. "Surfing instructor!"

"Yeah. Needless to say, Lena and I didn't communicate very well about today." Even as I mourned the loss of my one-on-one date with Daniel, I knew I had no choice. Stuart was family, and he looked hungry. "I'll go ask Olivia if you can both come! I'll just be a minute."

My minute with Olivia lengthened into fifteen, as it turned out she had just called Lena to offer her a job. Thrilled, I rushed back to convey the news to Stuart, all the while fearing that Daniel had given up on me and left.

I needn't have worried. The doors had opened, and the guys sat together at a table inside, talking like old friends at a reunion.

"We saved you a seat!" Stuart said.

"Gee, thanks." I got to have a seat at my own date.

"You didn't tell me you surfed." Daniel said it as if I'd been harboring a major secret from him.

"It didn't come up."

But my words went unheard. Daniel and Stuart had their heads together.

"Dude, you should come with us on Saturday, when Bree has her lesson." Stuart, his face creased into a big smile, looked excited by his own brilliant idea.

"Cool! Which beach do you go to?"

Hello! I'm right here, guys. Completely forgotten.

What if I didn't want Daniel to come on Saturday? What if I didn't want him to see my plump, neoprene-coated body splayed over a surfboard? I would have kicked Stuart in the leg, but Daniel was sitting between us, his back half-turned to me.

I would kick Stuart later.

"Shall we go get some food?" I said it as sweetly as possible. Olivia's small store opened out to a surprisingly spacious back patio, where tables with white linen tablecloths held all-white platters of finger foods, meticulously displayed. Shrimp, marinated olives, and pancetta-wrapped figs. Gingered pecans, miniature egg rolls, and cheeses with deliciously crusty homemade bread. On one large table: lemon bars, chocolate-covered strawberries, tiny fruit tarts, and tiramisu. Only the discreet piles of order forms with the name and price of each item of food served as a reminder that this was a working event.

It dawned on me that I'd been all wrong about today. I had pictured myself and Daniel hand-feeding each other delectable morsels selected for their aphrodisiac qualities. Instead, I would need to take notes and make decisions about what tasted best and what we could afford for our premiere. What on earth had made me think this was a date, anyway?

At least we had amazing food to eat. I would put the guys to work. "How about we take two plates each and collect everything that looks good to us? Mark down what you take on an order list. Then we come back to the table, and sample things together."

"I'm going to take one plate of food and count it as lunch," Daniel said as the three of us hovered over a tray of stuffed mushroom caps.

"Of course!" I shouldn't have been surprised that he had planned to eat mindfully today. He'd been doing it for over two years. My addicted mind, on the other hand, had already labeled this outing as a special exception, one where rules went out the window, because we were supposed to have fun, right?

"And I hope you don't mind—I don't eat sugar," he added.

How could anyone not eat sugar? Yet many of the program people didn't. "It's okay."

A server approached with a tray of wine glasses.

"No thank you." Stuart waved him away before Daniel and I had a chance to respond. "I've got over sixty days of abstinence from drugs and alcohol," he told Daniel. "No way am I screwing that up!"

I guess it didn't matter that I had to work, given I was in the company of saints. Or martyrs. I wasn't sure which.

To support Stuart, Daniel and I passed on the fine wines and drank only iced tea. Stuart did all my dessert sampling, while Daniel and I stuck with moderate amounts of the savory selections. It helped a lot having two other tasters with me. We sat with four large plates of tidbits (Stuart had taken two), sampling from all of them. If two of us disagreed on an item, a third would break the tie.

"I give the wontons an A, but the oysters a B plus," Stuart reported, while I made notes.

"The horseradish sauce is excellent on the mini-roast beef sandwiches," Daniel told me.

With their help, I made my menu for the party. "Thanks, you guys! This was fun!" And it had been, even though it hadn't gone anything like I expected. I wondered if I would ever have a real, live date with Daniel, the kind where no one else joined us.

"So next week? We'll see you at the beach?" Stuart spoke to Daniel as he said goodbye to the two of us.

"You bet!" Daniel opened his car door for me, I slid in, and he ran around to the other side. Stuart bent down to lean in my window. "Bye, you guys! Have fun on your date tonight, Bree!"

I felt Daniel tense up beside me. It was on the tip of my tongue to say, *Stuart's confused. I don't have a date tonight.* But then . . . I didn't. Let him wonder, like I'd wondered about Rachel. Men were supposed to like the chase, weren't they? Maybe I should give him one.

Twenty

Sitting in bed that evening, I stared at the calendar on my laptop, fighting off panic. What did it mean, when your heart fluttered erratically in your chest like a wounded butterfly? Was that normal, or were you having a heart attack? Now my breath was getting rapid and shallow. A pain pierced my right temple. Was I having a stroke?

I had decided it was time to take stock. Review my progress to date and reset my sights, if necessary. The results of my efforts were before me.

Weight: Had increased by seven pounds during my period of extended bingeing. Was now down six pounds due to mindful eating in recent weeks.

Net change in weight: A gain of one pound.

Amount of weight to lose: Forty-one pounds.

Time to completion: Six weeks left until D-Day. July 17, the date that I was to perform a miracle and simultaneously host parties on both coasts of our great nation.

New goal: Lose seven pounds a week over the next six weeks.

Clearly, I wasn't going to lose seven pounds a week.

I stared unseeingly at my pride and joy—the *Passion of Cecily* cover on my bedroom wall—and asked myself for the thousandth time: Why had I done this to myself?

A FaceTime call came in for me on Monday. "Sabrina? This is—"

"Hi, Candace!" From Candace's Book Blog. She had cut her hair very short, giving her a boyish look, and wore a T-shirt and overalls. Very different from the ethereal hippie-like creature of a month ago.

"You changed your look!"

"Yeah, I do that. Keeps people on their toes."

I found myself happy and terrorized in equal parts to hear from her once again. She'd been so nice to me during our failed interview, but I knew why she was calling. Remembering Candace as the sort of person who didn't waste time, I figured I'd better get to the point. "I haven't lost any weight."

"Not a problem! Did you buy clothes?"

I had obviously remembered her correctly.

"I got a dress."

"Awesome."

We booked a date and time for a second interview to replace the one I'd suffered through before. *Big help,* I thought. What was going to bail me out of all the suffering that lay ahead of me: the tight waistbands, trickling sweat, legs too chubby to cross? The secret devouring of calories that didn't fool anyone? The painful, omnipresent reality of being fat?

A thought floated through my mind.

You don't have to be fat. Not if you purge.

Candace had been the one to say it. It seemed too good to be true, but she had the trim body to back up her claim.

I once again gave a silent thank-you that Josh was in Texas, allowing me to conduct secret conversations in the privacy of an empty office. "Candace? You know how to purge, right?"

Slowly: "Yeah, why?"

"Is it hard to learn?"

She squinted out at me from the screen of my laptop. "Not really. I taught a bunch of my sorority sisters in college."

"Would you show me? I'm not sure how you get it to work."

"Why do you want to know?"

I decided I'd been wrong about the time-wasting thing. Candace was doing a pretty good job of it right now. "I'm curious. It just seems like a good way to keep the weight off. You know, if you binge a lot."

She gave a heavy sigh. "Just stick your finger in your mouth."

"I've tried that. Is there a special trick to it?" I stuck my index finger in my mouth and wiggled it around, with no result.

"Lemme see." Candace peered intently out in my direction.

I opened my mouth wider, shoving it up close to the screen to provide clear viewing, and waggled my finger some more.

"Not like that! You have to touch the back of your throat," Candace said, "and keep it there a minute."

I tried again, plunging my finger into my throat while Candace yelled, "Do it again!" Then I choked and spat. Finally, gagging, I jerked my hand out of my mouth.

"I give up!" There had to be another way to lose weight fast.

Candace's eyebrows knit themselves together. "Maybe," she ventured, her voice cracking, "it's just as well."

"But if I could get thin this way . . ."

Her chin began to tremble. "To be honest, purging's kind of a suckfest. Really. I don't recommend it."

In my heart, I knew she was right. "Nothing works! Isn't there something else I could try?"

"Well, there might be one thing," Candace said slowly.

And she told me.

Wiping my nose and punching the keys with stiff fingers, I typed a word into Google and scrolled down the search results. The word was *liposuction*.

My eyes fastened themselves on a name. Dr. Evangeline Yee of Beverly Hills. I clicked on her website, which featured a picture of a small bespectacled woman in a pristine white coat standing with a group of happy patients. Before-and-after photos confirmed that Dr. Yee could change a hook nose into a ski slope, create a chin where there'd been none before, and pare away excess adipose like a chef slicing the fat off a ham. A master of fat removal, Dr. Yee had performed over sixteen thousand liposuction procedures. She was just what I needed.

Dr. Yee's website was full of good information. Traditional liposuction, I read, was about removing little pockets of fat off a relatively thin person. They had something now, though, called large volume liposuction. That was when they took an obese person and just vacuumed out all her fat—up to five liters of it. As a trailblazer in the field of cosmetic surgery, Dr. Yee naturally provided this valuable service.

According to the doctor's website, a patient could undergo large volume liposuction and be back to work in a week and fully recovered within four to six weeks. That could potentially fit my schedule.

It was almost like a modern-day fairy tale. Just as Sleeping Beauty had dozed off and woke up with an awesome boyfriend, I could go to sleep and wake up thin. With Dr. Yee as my fairy godmother.

But how much did it cost? That information was nowhere on the website.

I'd have to call tomorrow. Hope rose in the air and circled around me. This could be it. If I could afford it, the answer to my problems.

Twenty-One

Eight thousand five hundred dollars. That was the price attached to Dr. Yee's services. I would have to sacrifice my entire advance and run both my credit cards up to the hilt. Including my student loans, I would then be $58,500 in debt, with no end in sight.

But worth it, if it made me skinny, right? Because then my life would be perfect.

Sitting cross-legged on my bed, I was working from home today, a luxury permitted by Corinne's unfortunate illness. A ding from my laptop announced a new email. When I saw it was from Kaitlyn, I didn't have the strength to open it.

What was I going to do?

I found myself putting a text in to Michelle. *You have a moment?*
Sure what's up?

What *was* up? I didn't know exactly why I'd reached out to her. A big bubble of pain was rising in my chest and expanding, filling my rib cage and pressing on my heart. My breathing turned fast and shallow. My eyes burned. I texted back to her.

I need help.

A pause, and then the little dots came up, indicating she was typing. *Hold that thought.*

A second later, my phone rang. "Sabrina? What's happening?"

I wasn't sure. "It's just that . . . my editor wants me to go New York and wear this red dress . . . but I can't walk down a staircase looking like that . . . and I tried to barf, but then I couldn't . . . and I can't afford liposuction—"

"*Liposuction?* Hold on a sec . . ." Scrabbling noises and the shriek of an outraged toddler. Michelle's muffled voice. "You get one book each. Mackenzie already chose that one." Her voice came back to me. "I'm at work, but I can meet you for lunch. Can you keep it together until then?"

I nodded, then realized she couldn't see me. "Yes."

Thumping noises and crying, followed by a blur of speech.

"What?" I asked.

"Not you. I'll meet you at the Coffee Station at noon. And in the meantime, here's an assignment. Pretend that you believe in God and decide exactly what you'd want that God to be like. Your perfect higher power. Then, write him a letter. And then, write his response to you." Another shriek. "I should go."

This was what she had to suggest? A letter to God? Stifling my doubts, I said, "Okay. I'll see you at noon."

Dear God, I wrote. Then I stopped. The pain bubble had returned, punishing me for all the mistakes of recent weeks. As a further rebuke, I had to write this silly letter to God.

I forced myself to go on.

You don't know me, but my name is Sabrina Hunter. Although, if you were my perfect God, I guess you'd already know who I am. So I should say instead: Sabrina Hunter here, just checking in.

Damn straight he should know who I was. That is, if he were all-powerful and all-knowing. I forged ahead.

Now that I think about it, you must know who I am, because you're the one who made me, right? If that's true, I have a few questions for you. Like, for example, how come my sister tans when I only freckle? And how come she gets full after half a chocolate chip cookie when I always have to eat the entire box?

I was rolling now. I mean, really. Why was God so unfair? Why did some people get everything and others nothing?

And why do sad things happen? Is it to give us perspective so we appreciate the good things more? Is it to punish us for our failings (which you created, I have to point out).

The pain bubble expanded. You'd think God would be kinder. You'd think he'd protect people a little.

It doesn't seem fair that people have to suffer. Why do young people have to die, and why do people fall out of love? Why do parents leave their children?

I stopped writing, not sure where my outburst had come from. This was no way to ingratiate myself with God, if he were in fact up there somewhere. And it was way too personal and sincere to share with Michelle. I deleted everything I'd written and started over.

Dear God,

Sabrina Hunter here, but you can call me Bree ha ha. I've never written you a letter before, so this is a bit of an experiment.

Actually, this wasn't my idea. My sponsor is making me write to you because I want to get liposuction. I shouldn't have gotten her going on the liposuction because I can't afford it anyway.

But you can make anything happen, right, God? So here's the thing. My one burning short-term need is to lose forty pounds in the next five weeks. Beyond that, I would just like to be able to eat normally and stay at a normal weight. I would also like to make my living by writing books. And I would like to date Daniel.

I stopped and reread what I had, then deleted the sentence about Daniel. Michelle would see this, after all.

Could you arrange any of those things for me? I try to be a good person, so I hope you'll take that into account.

Sincerely yours,

Sabrina Hunter

Now for the response. I imagined God was busy and would keep it short and sweet.

Dear Sabrina,

Thank you for your letter. I will take your request into consideration and get back to you within two to three weeks.

Warmest regards,

God

I reread it. This might not be the kind of thing Michelle had in mind. Maybe I should try another approach, something a little less . . . flippant. Something more from the heart. But a tiny worm of stubbornness squirmed inside me. What did God and weight loss have to do with each other? It didn't make sense.

The letter was authentically me, I would give it that much. I would go with it.

Michelle won't like this, a small voice said. But the little worm, the one that said, *I don't want to do this,* poked its head up again. I would put the decision off and distract myself with Kaitlyn's email.

My computer hummed and clicked while I called it up. As I read it, my blood froze.

> *Sabrina! I can't believe I forgot this. I should have asked weeks ago, so now it's a rush. We need current photos of you for the jacket cover and promotional pieces. A couple of headshots or one head and one body shot, but as soon as you can! Thanks!*

Throw me to a python so that I may be strangled inch by infinitesimal inch. Maybe I would tell Kaitlyn that I didn't want my face shown for security reasons, that I wanted to protect my anonymity. Maybe I'd deny getting her email. Maybe I just wouldn't think about it right now.

I lurched to my feet. It was time to meet Michelle for lunch. I would show her the God letters as is. What did it matter, anyway?

Michelle looked up after reading my letters, her expression carefully neutral. "I was hoping you'd take this seriously." She took a sip from her cappuccino mug. Today, she wore a bright pink athletic suit with navy trim. Her hair stood in little fluffs around her face, which drooped with . . . something. Fatigue, maybe, or worry.

Thinking of those snarky letters made my cheeks red. I hoped she didn't think I'd disrespected her, this kind person who, at my request, had agreed to help me. "I'm sorry," I said. "I just have a lot on my mind right now."

And with that, I poured out the whole story. The book, my dreams, Fast Track, the red dress, the impending July 17 fiasco. The only thing I left out was Daniel. "So I've got all this weight to lose in a short time. And I thought . . . maybe liposuction . . ." I trailed off. "But I don't have the money."

"Thank goodness for that!" Michelle's eyebrows knitted together in distress. "I can't tell you what to do about your weight loss emergency. Our program is designed for the long haul. It takes a lot of commitment." She stopped speaking, and I could sense her reluctance to push me. "Maybe you're not ready for it."

"Don't say that!" The words flew out of my mouth, surprising me. Even more surprising was the stab of pain I'd felt when I heard them. Talk about getting a vote of no confidence.

Right then and there, I made up my mind. "I do want to be in the program. I don't have anywhere else to go." Only at the program could I get the kind of amazing support I needed to cure this illness, if that's what it was, this compulsion to eat no matter what, even if I was sick from overeating, even if it distorted my body and ruined my life.

Plus, I liked the program. I liked the kind, friendly people, who all suffered from the same strange obsession that I did. People who profoundly believed in the program but went about it quietly, without selling it or trying to convert the nonbelievers. To do that would be to lack humility, to presume that you knew better than another person how that person should live his life.

"It's true," Michelle said. "There's no other place to go. For us, anyway. Most of us know that because we've tried everything else."

Unshed tears burned in my eyes. "So what should I do next?"

"Keep following your food plan, for one thing. And share at the next meeting you go to." She must have seen me gear up to protest, because she stopped me short. "It's good for you. And you also need to clean up your mess at work. You'll never have any peace until you get straight with your editor and resolve that July seventeenth problem."

She was right.

"Thanks," I told her. Something in her expression made me scrutinize her closely, the blue rings under her eyes, the discouraged droop of her shoulders. "Are you okay?"

Her lips trembled. "It's been rough. I lost a baby a few days back. It was only seven weeks along, but we were so excited."

I sat back, shocked. "I'm so sorry." Here I was whining about my little problems, while she, who had just suffered the greatest loss imaginable, had come to help me. "I'm such a jerk."

She shook her head. "Don't feel that way. It does me good to be of service in my spare time. I feel better talking to you than moping around."

"No, really, I've been so insensitive."

"*Don't,*" she said, her voice hardening. "Don't make this all about you."

It was as if I'd been slapped. "Okay." Mortified, I stared at the table.

Michelle reached out and grasped my hand, and we sat for a moment like that.

Finally, I spoke. "Thanks, Michelle. For helping me like this."

"You're welcome." A small smile twisted the corner of her lip. "You can do this. The key is to keep coming back. No matter what happens, no matter how many times you screw up, keep coming back."

"Okay."

"And remember, one day at a time."

Keep coming back.

One day at a time.

I would remember.

Twenty-Two

A nother Thursday night meeting, and I had promised Michelle I would share. "It's good for you," she'd insisted.

I doubted that. Sharing was public speaking, which left you exposed and vulnerable. It required being seen. It gave you one chance to get your thoughts out there, and if you blew it, it was all over.

Writing was so much better. I could craft and recraft my thoughts until they were perfect, then hide in the shadows while someone else read them.

For the first time, I hoped Daniel wouldn't come to the meeting. I sat in the second row, waiting for it to start. I'd had a highly annoying, but ultimately successful day with Alexa Fredericks, the proof of it being the signed contract safely filed back at the office. I'd left a jubilant message for Josh, but he hadn't called back.

Josh was hard to reach these days, and when I did reach him, he was busy torturing the Texas medical community—haranguing nurses and making demands of Corinne's doctors even as he spoke to me on the phone. I was glad he was far away. But a little part of me wondered what it would be like to love and live with someone like Corinne. I didn't envy Josh his life.

And now Daniel was rushing in at the last minute, looking all grown up in a sports jacket, button-down white shirt, and tan slacks.

He carried a bulky lawyer's briefcase made of rich, dark leather. Seeing an empty chair beside me, he made his way over to sit with me. I noted with a thrill of excitement that to get to me, he had to climb over three people, briefcase and all, when he could have easily taken a seat on the aisle.

Even to me, it seemed as if he liked me. Normally, I didn't think anyone liked me, especially not attractive men. With jobs. And all their parts and faculties intact.

"Hi," he said in my ear. "Just came from court." He had settled back for the meeting, or at least, as well as one could into a metal folding chair, while I perched on mine, unable to relax. I was conscious of his breathing and the way his elbow occasionally brushed against mine. And if I survived this meeting, I would get to hold his hand again at the very end.

This week's leader told her story. "I'm Jennifer, compulsive overeater. I've been eating mindfully on the program for seventeen years. I've learned to put the program first, ahead of my husband, my kids, my job. If I do, I can be there for the people I love. If I don't, I'm no good to anyone."

After she finished speaking, it was time for members to share. Quivering, I forced my hand up. Jennifer called on someone in the first row.

Whew. Off the hook for the next three minutes, but it turned out that three minutes went by really fast when you were using them to procrastinate. The first share ended, and I raised my hand again. Jennifer nodded toward me.

Showtime.

"Hi. I'm Sabrina, compulsive overeater."

"Hi, Sabrina," the group chorused back.

The bubble of pain expanded in my chest again; my throat and eyes burned. "So . . . I'm still really new to the program. This is my first share *ever*."

That comment drew sympathetic laughter and applause.

"I'm trying to eat mindfully, and my sponsor's helping me. But the concept of a higher power is still really foreign to me." I stopped for a second. My rib cage filled with a burning pain that left me short of breath. My head throbbed. I felt myself sliding toward a babbling meltdown. *Oh, God, here I go.*

"My mother left us when I was nine," I blurted. "My sister was five." I hadn't meant to say that. It just came out. "She went away and never came back."

All rustling and movement in the room had stopped. The meeting members sat quietly, listening to my story.

"My dad went kind of crazy. He disappeared for two days, leaving us alone in the house. It turned out he was off looking for Mom, but we didn't know that. We thought they had both left us forever. We stayed by ourselves in that house for two days and nights, and I had to take care of my little sister. I was so scared. We ate bread and peanut butter from the pantry and hid under my parents' bed at night in case a monster or a bad man came to kill us. We were too scared to sleep in our own beds."

I stopped talking, only to realize that tears were pouring down my face. "Then, Dad came back. He told us that he'd seen Mom. She was going to live in Atlanta from now on. She was marrying another man and didn't plan to come visit us.

"My dad had never been openly loving, but after that, he became even more withdrawn and was always working. He hired this housekeeper who did nothing, and he didn't notice. She didn't bother to buy groceries half the time, and I had to ask him to do it. Or he'd bring us dinner after work, except he wouldn't come home until nine o'clock, and we'd be so hungry waiting for him."

My eyes rained tears, and I sniffled loudly. "I don't understand why a good and loving God would let that happen to my sister and me, or to any kid. I don't get it." I just barely choked out the last words, then sobbed aloud.

I felt a soft pressure in my hand and heard a woman's voice in my ear. "Keep it," she said. I was holding the prettiest handkerchief I'd ever seen. In a soft cotton printed with flowers and hearts, it had a faint scent of orange blossoms, maybe, or jasmine. I turned to thank the woman next to me, but she shook her head. "It's from over there," she whispered, pointing to the far end of the room. Apparently, it had been passed along hand to hand. Whoever it came from had blended back into the group of twenty or so men and women in attendance.

I clutched the beautiful handkerchief as if it were a life preserver. It was way too pretty to cry on, so I wiped my nose on my sleeve.

"Thanks for listening," I said, then sobbed again as the timer dinged, indicating my three minutes were up. While another share started, I continued to cry, completely unhinged except for the dim awareness of a pleasant sensation that turned out to be Daniel's arm around my shoulder.

As the meeting closed, we stood and formed a circle, and Daniel reached for my hand and held it through the prayer. I would have been ecstatic, except that I'd been sniveling into that hand for the last twenty minutes. I hoped he wasn't too grossed out by it.

After the prayer came the weekly closing cheer. Squeezing each other's hands hard and pumping them up and down, we exclaimed together, "Keep coming back! It works if you work it, and you're worth it!"

As we milled around, members approached me.

"I loved your share! I completely related to it!"

"I was so moved by your story!"

"What you said meant a lot to me."

"Thank you!" It had never occurred to me that my story and experiences could be meaningful to someone else. I hoped the handkerchief lady would identify herself, but no one came forward. Surreptitiously, I tucked the pretty handkerchief into a pocket of my purse. I would keep it with me for luck.

I walked out of the meeting room with Daniel close behind, not looking back, not daring to let him see my still running nose and red eyes. Outside, he pulled up beside me and put his hand on my back as we walked along. "You okay?"

I nodded, keeping my eyes down. "Yeah. I didn't mean to get so emotional."

"Everybody does it."

"Really? They do?"

"Sure. That's what meetings are for."

We reached my car. Daniel leaned against the driver's door, making it impossible for me to open. His slouching brought his eyes—and lips—just about level with mine.

"There's a place down the road with great Irish coffee. It's just the thing after an emotional share." The corner of his mouth quirked up and his eyes warmed.

I stared at him. Was he asking me to go for a drink? Or just imparting useful information? I didn't think I could survive another moment of total mortification around Daniel.

In the face of my silence, he leaned forward. "Do you want to go?"

"Oh! Yes. Please."

"Great. We'll take my car, and I'll bring you back here afterward."

It was an Irish bar with dark wooden booths accessorized with all-green napkins, plates, and wall shamrocks. The servers wore matching green T-shirts. At the bar, burly guys shouted at some sporting event on the TV, while signs advertised turtle races, which, mercifully, were on another night.

We took a small booth and sat across from each other nursing our coffees. A self-consciousness lay over us now that we were in new territory. Before, we'd always seen each other in circumstances you could write off as non-dates. Program meetings or events. Chance encounters or group outings.

But this time, he'd asked me to have a drink with him—alone and for no reason except he wanted my company. In the evening—another good sign. All that was left was the matter of who paid the bill. If he paid, this would meet all the parameters of a real date.

We would see.

"So, Stuart's going to marry your sister?" he said.

"Yeah. It's going to be really small, which was supposed to make it simple and easy . . ."

"But it's not? Simple and easy, that is?" he asked.

"No. Problematic family dynamics on both sides."

Daniel scratched his head. "I'm not sure what's worse, problematic family dynamics, or nonexistent."

"Nonexistent?"

"Well, my parents and the aunt who raised my brothers, Luke and Philip, are dead. There are no other important adults to speak of, so it's just me and the twins."

"Are they really close?" I asked.

"Yeah, very."

Where did that leave Daniel? He spoke matter-of-factly, yet I couldn't help but feel he was all alone in the world. "What about girlfriends?" The question slipped out before I could stop myself.

He gave a startled laugh. "Contrary to what you might think, I don't have a girlfriend right now."

I plucked up my courage. "I kind of thought you were dating Rachel."

"Not anymore, and she was never a girlfriend."

"But you had girlfriends before her?"

"Well, sure."

"Really?" Again, the question popped out of me. "Like . . . when?" I added, flushing painfully. Did I have to sound so surprised that he'd had girls in his younger life?

Daniel shook his head and laughed at me. "Like, in high school. And college. And law school . . . What?" he added teasingly. "You didn't think a big guy could get any action?"

I threw caution to the wind. "I'm sure *you* could have."

And then I was drowning in a sea of glorious blue-flecked-with-green eye contact, the way only Daniel could deliver it. Nothing, I thought, could be better, but I was wrong.

He reached out and took my hand. "You're really something, Sabrina Hunter."

Holy hotness! In a split second, I'd been transported into a state of perfect bliss, a place where I could happily have pitched a tent and stayed forever.

His hand was deliciously warm and, interestingly, both hard and soft to touch. He intertwined his fingers with mine, while I fought the urge to kick my leg up and down like a dog getting his belly scratched. He continued to hold my hand while we talked about the program and my job and how I'd gotten Alexa to sign the contract, and finally we let go of each other's hands to drink our Irish coffees, which were getting cold. The coffees were good, but holding hands was better.

"So tell me about your job," I said.

He brightened. "Well, actually," he said, "I was able to bring a really interesting case into the office." He took a sip of his coffee. "It means travel to Miami and Central America, plus nonstop work for the next few months. But it's a dream case, a really important immigration case—one that could go to the Supreme Court!"

"That's fantastic!" I said, thinking, *This guy is so cool.* I liked a guy with ambition, a high achiever, maybe because I was ambitious too.

People at the bar were cheering for the game on the TV while customers and servers passed our table, but all of that was only the dimmest of backgrounds for me. I was acutely aware of Daniel's voice, his smile, his way of leaning toward me as we continued to talk.

He took my hand again and held it while I told him about the new book I was writing. "It's called *The Heartbreak of Cecily.* It's the follow-up to the book being published right now, so this first book just has to sell. Otherwise, number two'll never see the light of day."

Daniel nodded emphatically. "You'll do it! Have confidence!" We continued to talk, and he told me what it was like to lose eighty pounds and become, in the eyes of others at least, a totally different person.

Right about the time they began to mop the floors, we realized it was midnight.

I felt like I was emerging from a dimly lit dream place into the blinding bright light of reality. It took me a few seconds to adjust. "It's gonna be tough to get up tomorrow morning."

Daniel took the check.

"How much do I owe you?" I asked.

Daniel shook his head. "I got this."

It *was*. It was a date! "Thank you." I said it as demurely as I could.

We walked out to his car and drove back to mine, chatting about our upcoming surfing expedition and the next softball game. The few silences that came up were comfortable.

"You're not going to go home and answer interview questions, are you?" Daniel asked as we pulled up to my car. "You put me to shame!"

"No all-nighters today. Thanks for the drink and the company."

And then he put his arms around me and kissed me. Not just one kiss, either. He took his time, kissing me for a few perfect moments, like the true high achiever he was.

Finally, he released me.

"Bye." Breathless and dreamy, I gazed at him, cow-eyed.

"Bye," he said. "See you soon. I'll call you."

Twenty-Three

He didn't call for three days, during which I suffered the agonies of the damned, obsessing over him and Hostess cupcakes in roughly equal amounts. I texted Michelle incessantly, supposedly for program support, but actually for any snippets of news she might have about Daniel. When he finally called at 6:00 P.M. on Saturday, his tired voice grated against my ears.

"Sabrina? I'm in Miami. The day after I saw you, our team took off on four hours' notice, and we've been in depositions ever since."

"Are you coming home soon?" Such a relief to hear from him and to know he had a good excuse for ignoring me.

"Doubtful. We've got a whole room full of boxes with documents to go through."

We only talked a few minutes and hung up with no plans for speaking with or seeing each other again.

The following week, I thought all the time of Daniel but still managed to run the office in Josh's absence, eat my three healthy meals a day, go to meetings, and talk to Michelle. "It's funny," I told her. "The food part's been easier this week. I haven't craved sweets and snacks. I've enjoyed some of my meals. Does this mean I'm recovered?"

"If you were able to stay in that place, then yes. But most of us move in and out of serenity, especially at the beginning."

Serenity. In program-speak, it meant freedom from food obsession. You had food three times a day, and in between meals, you lived your life. You didn't devote all your thoughts and energy to the next meal. You didn't steal candy, dream of chocolate, eat potato chips in your car. In your dealings with people, you were "present," meaning you were engaged, listening and speaking to them in the moment, instead of reacting from the depths of your addiction or some graveyard of buried pain.

All this you achieved even if the rest of your life was a steaming pile of excrement. That was the key, that even with many reasons to lose control and binge, you'd stopped needing the compulsive behavior. You'd found other ways to cope.

Serenity. It was bliss. I'd even lost two pounds.

But as Michelle had hinted, it wouldn't last forever.

Sabrina,

Thank you for all those interview answers—done fast and well, as you seem to do everything. That was a grisly job, so brava!

But . . .

And here she'd put in two emojis wearing puzzled expressions . . .

I've received no photos from you. I need them pronto! Surely you have something we can use. Please get right on it.

Kaitlyn

Poison me. Let me die slowly and painfully.

So, I'd lost two pounds. Big deal. I had only thirty-eight more to lose in the next four weeks, almost five pounds a week.

I had to face facts. I couldn't put off telling her any longer.

It was Saturday morning, and Stuart, Lena, Twinkie, and I were headed for the beach in Stuart's vintage Lincoln, a behemoth with the cushy ride of a giant airborne Tempur-Pedic mattress. A while back, I'd thought Daniel might respond to Stuart's invitation and come along, but now he was in Miami, as far as I knew. I hadn't heard from him in five days.

This morning, I did my hair and put on blush and mascara so that just in case Daniel came, I could wow him in the ten dry minutes I would have with him before we plunged into the Pacific Ocean. But all of that would only help from the neck up. The rest of me I would have to hide behind an artfully positioned surfboard.

Stuart spun the wheel of his cruisemobile, floating it into the almost empty parking lot. We got a great spot next to the beach entrance, our reward for being early birds. Already I was looking around for Daniel's car. The day was gorgeous. The sun shone, and a breeze whipped the ocean into tiny whitecaps. Only a couple of surfers dotted the water this early.

Then I remembered my dilemma. "What'm I gonna do about Kaitlyn?" I moaned from the back seat. Stuart stared over his shoulder at me as he put on the parking brake. "Total honesty," he pronounced. "Moral integrity." They were principles of the program.

I looked to Lena for support as we climbed out of the car, but I should have known she would side with Stuart. Standing there in the parking lot, he and I began to pull on our wet suits.

"You've got to tell your editor what's going on. As soon as possible." Lena was leashing up Twinkie for their walk.

"You ready? Let's go!" Stuart had our boards out and was already looking eagerly toward the ocean.

"I guess Daniel couldn't make it." My eyes swept the parking lot again.

"I know. He texted me."

"He did?"

"He's working. He flew his team down to Costa Rica."

"Why didn't you tell me?"

"I'm telling you now."

Daniel had told Stuart about it, but not me. I reminded myself that Stuart was the one who'd invited him. Of course Daniel would get in touch with him. And he knew Stuart would tell me, so why send two texts when one would do?

We trudged across the sand, lugging our boards. I panted as I pulled my feet over and over from the deep sand and staggered forward with my heavy load. Grumpiness set in. This part of surfing was by far my least favorite. In fact, this part of surfing was a pain in the ass.

Plus, Daniel's failure to communicate was messing with my mind. I had to admit it: I was miffed. Apparently, I didn't matter enough to deserve a text, let alone a phone call.

Finally, we reached the water. I glared out toward the horizon, lost in my own thoughts.

"Bree? Y'all set?" Stuart gave me an inquiring look. With his wet suit, blond ponytail, dark tan, and seashell necklace, he looked like a beautiful Polynesian-Viking God.

A phrase came to mind: "Drowning my sorrows." That's what I would do. Drown my sorrows.

"Yeah. I'm ready," I told him.

I threw myself into the ocean.

For two hours, I expelled all thought from my head and pitted myself against the waves. Each one was a rival to be taken down, a challenge to be met. After coaching me through the first few, Stuart stopped teaching and started surfing with me. We would paddle out to where the waves were breaking and wait, poised to catch the oncoming wave at just the right time. I stayed slightly behind Stuart, studying him and matching his movements—the way he took his time on the pop-up, crouching low on the board, and getting his balance before he stood. Soon I was doing it consistently.

What a rush! To ride right in the pocket of the wave, to feel the power of the water, the speed, the movement of my feet on the board. I forgot about my weight, the mistakes I'd made, the grudges I'd nursed, my petty complaints. I was living life minute by minute, and right now, right here, this minute was heaven.

I hated to stop, and I could tell Stuart did too. "Dude, you were sick," he told me as we set off for the car. "You crushed it."

When we got there, Lena took one look at me and said, "Hold it right there, missy!" Using her phone, she took my picture, then checked it and grinned. "This one's a keeper."

She showed it to me. My wet hair slicked back like a seal's, I stood framed by the ocean and beach behind me, my brightly colored surfboard at my side. Yes, I was alarmingly spherical in my wet suit, but my eyes glowed and my cheeks bloomed with color. I looked like someone you'd want to know, someone vibrant and fully alive.

Even I couldn't complain about the shot. "Would you text that to me?"

"Of course."

As we drove home, I ditched my seat belt and lay in the expansive back seat looking up at the sky. It was illegal, but as long as I stayed low, the cops wouldn't see me. Lying there, I idly tried to daydream up for myself some new careers in the event that I quit Josh and Fast Track blew me out of the water.

Maybe I could teach surfing, if I got really good at it. I could bartend, but no . . . I didn't want to go back to school. I guess that also ruled out architecture and veterinary medicine.

I had to face it. The only thing I'd ever wanted to do was write. Fast Track had given me that chance, and I was screwing it up. *Get your act together, Sabrina.*

I knew what I had to do. No more bullshitting. No more denial. When I got home, I pulled out my laptop and started an email.

Dear Kaitlyn,

Attached is a photo my sister took today at the beach. Maybe it's not the usual kind of photo one would use for a book jacket, but it's me. Let me know if you think it's okay.

Now for the worst part. Sweat broke out on my forehead even as I gathered my courage. I would keep it short and simple.

Also, with regard to the red dress in my website photo, I'm afraid it is on hiatus until such time as I lose a bit of weight. Don't worry. I will wear a different dress to the launch party!

I'm really looking forward to meeting you next month. Thanks so much for believing in me and my book.

Best regards,

Sabrina

I crossed my fingers for a second, then attached the photograph and clicked send.

Then I waited. The fact that it was Saturday was not necessarily relevant, as I was dealing with Kaitlyn, the perpetual motion machine. Of course, technically I was working too, although in my case, it seemed less like work than a desperate attempt at survival.

I hoped it would all be okay. They wouldn't void my contract, would they? Could they do that? I mean, I had rights too, under the contract. Or did I?

It was too much to process. I'd eaten my lunch of tuna salad and tomato slices and strawberries recently enough that I couldn't claim actual physical hunger. That's why I knew that the sudden vision of a chocolate chip cookie ice cream sandwich was just a craving. It pulsed temptingly in the air before my eyes. I pushed it away, only to see it replaced by a pile of warm, sticky cinnamon buns. I could smell them. I could see one in my hand, watch myself finding the end and slowly pulling to unroll the pastry, revealing the powdery cinnamon inside.

But I didn't binge.

All that evening and all day Sunday, I continued to hallucinate about food while I waited to hear from Kaitlyn. I told myself that instead of seeing food, I should picture her ideal response. If I visualized it with crystal clarity, I would make it happen.

Hi, Sabrina, she would write. *That photo is just perfect, and you don't look a bit overweight. I'm sure that you will look lovely to the spectators below as you come down a floating staircase in a tablecloth. We'll sell bunches of books! Toodles, Kaitlyn.*

No text. No phone call. The woman had worked every weekend since I'd known her. *Now* she was taking a few days off? She was probably waiting until Monday morning to call the legal department, who would point out a weight maintenance clause in the contract. Or whatever it was they called it. Kaitlyn would heave a huge sigh of relief and send me packing.

Because they'd made a mistake the first time around. My book wasn't, had never been, good enough. And neither was I.

I was mediocre, a wannabe. I didn't have the chops to write a book worth reading.

Just as Daniel hadn't seen fit to call me again after our one and only date. I wasn't fun or pretty enough to keep his interest.

Or to keep my mother's interest, for that matter. Or my dad's.

I just wasn't good enough. I never would be.

Twenty-Four

Monday morning came, and by 10:00 A.M. Pacific time, which meant 1:00 P.M. Eastern time, I'd still heard nothing from Kaitlyn. She was probably in the Fast Track legal department right now, arguing for immediate termination of my contract. What else might she do? Put me on an editorial blacklist so no one would ever work with me again? Hang my photo in the subways with warning signs? ROGUE AUTHOR! PRONE TO UNAUTHORIZED WEIGHT GAINS!

As my anxiety spiraled out of control, my food cravings did too. How did that line go in *The Night Before Christmas*? "Visions of sugar plums danced in my head." Food was dancing in my head, all right. I daydreamed of warm corn bread with honey and butter, slabs of English toffee, s'mores with real fire-roasted marshmallows and bits of chocolate—not anything fancy, but just good old-fashioned Hershey bars.

"You did the right thing," Michelle said during my regular morning phone check-in with her. "That's all you can do. The rest of it's up to your higher power."

"All I wanna do is eat."

"You're doing great. Try something new, like meditation. Or make outreach calls to other members." Her voice changed just enough so that I knew she was smiling. "Write another letter to God."

"Maybe I should." I wished I could make an outreach call to Daniel, but I didn't feel right about asking him to drop everything, in his current situation, to help me out. He had texted me three days ago.

Hey, Bree. Still working 24/7 here. Hope you're well.

It was, I told myself, better than nothing.

Barely.

The guy never took a break? Ever? I was sure he'd completely forgotten our Night of Romance. Forgotten our hands touching, the deep, sexy looks into each other's eyes, and—oh, God—those kisses, which were burned into my memory. It was enough to make a girl go postal. Even my troubles with *The Passion of Cecily* paled in comparison.

Well, no, they didn't. That's how important *Cecily* was to me. But the fact that Daniel even came close to her in my priorities showed how awesome he was, how much he was starting to matter.

My phone rang. Lena's voice rose high above her usual pitch. "Um. Can you come over here tonight?"

"Okay," I said slowly, trying to place the odd tone to her voice. "What's up?"

"I'd just like you to come over and talk to someone."

I heard a man's voice in the background and felt a shiver go through me. "Who's that?" I demanded, although I already knew.

Lena sighed. "It's Dad, okay? I'd like you to talk to Dad."

I let a silence lengthen between us.

"Please, Bree? For me?"

"All right," I said, knowing nothing good would come of it.

Twenty-Five

The first thing I noticed was his hair had gone from gray to white in the two years since I'd seen him last. This served only to make him even more handsome. My dad was one of those guys who looked better and better with age. If you spliced together George Clooney and Clint Eastwood and made the resulting person a salesman of obstetrical supplies, that would be my father.

He stood up from the purple sofa as I walked into Lena and Stuart's living room. "Sabrina." A light note of caution entered his voice. "It's good to see you."

No sign that he really meant it. Ignoring his move in my direction, I perched stiffly on the edge of an armchair and stared at a far corner. "Hi, Dad."

Stuart brought in a plate of celery and carrot sticks with what I knew would be a fat-free dressing. He winked at me. "For you!"

"You're my hero!" I beamed at him. Lena had gotten a good one, a real peach, that was for sure.

Lena came in behind Stuart. She wore a sundress and over it an orange apron with a cheerful yellow sunflower on it. I suddenly flashed to another time when I'd seen that sunflower, many years ago. That had been my mother's apron. Seeing it on Lena now was unsettling.

She carried a tray and had curled her hair into ringlets that fell down around her bare shoulders. Her tray sent off an aroma that was familiar, but not entirely pleasant. I wrinkled my nose, trying to place it.

With a flourish, Lena set the tray on her Mercedes wheel coffee table. "Look what I made, guys!" She stepped back, her face so hopeful that a pang of affection for her shot through my heart, only to end when I saw her offering.

Pigs in blankets—little hot dogs wrapped in pieces of store-bought puff pastry.

I couldn't believe it. Mom used to make them for Dad and us on special occasions—they were our favorite treats. After she took off, we never had them again. In the beginning, I was too young to make them, and by the time I was old enough, I hated my mother way too much to rekindle any part of our past together. And now Lena had made them, as if they were part of some treasured, shared memory between us.

"Remember, Dad?" she said as he leaned forward to peruse the tray.

"Yes." He took one of the appetizers and held it for a moment in a napkin, then sighed heavily, setting it on the side table next to him. A memory came back to me of Dad's face, etched in lines of grief, after Mom's departure.

"Bree? Stuart?" Striving for normalcy, Lena handed each of us one of the little dogs in a napkin. My throat closing up at the sight of them, I sat with mine in my hand.

"Don't mind if I do." Stuart wolfed his down and helped himself to a second.

Dad had written to Mom and called her for months, trying to persuade her to return. It was almost as if Lena and I didn't exist, or existed solely to prevent him from getting her back.

Stuart walked over and sat down on the sofa beside Lena, casually putting a protective arm around her. My eyes misted over. Stuart was Team Lena, all the way.

Well, so was I. I'd stood by Lena all my life, and I wasn't going to stop now.

She pulled and twisted one of her ringlets, flattening it. "Stuart and I have some news!"

"More news than the fact that you're getting married?" I asked.

She gasped, giving me a reproachful look. "That was supposed to be a surprise for Dad!"

It was my turn to gasp. "I'm so sorry! I assumed you'd told him!"

"No, I didn't." Smiling nervously, she turned toward him for his reaction.

At that moment, we heard a ringtone, and Dad was pulling out his cell. "Hang on," he said to Lena. He turned his back on her, one finger in his ear.

"That's not good enough," he said. "Let me talk to him." He walked out of the room.

"Must be an important call," Stuart said soothingly to Lena, whose smile had vanished. "Here, Twinkie needs a petting!" He called the dog over, picked him up, and gave him to Lena, who stroked his face and ears.

We listened while Dad's voice ground on in the next room, then finally stopped. He emerged, shaking his head. "Idiots! I have to do everything!" He did a double take when he saw Lena holding Twinkie. "When did you get a dog?"

"Dad!" I yelled, steaming mad. "Did you hear what Lena just said? She's getting married!"

Dad walked over to Lena. "Congratulations," he said, shaking Stuart's hand and pulling Lena into a stiff hug. "This is wonderful news."

He'd made no effort to speak to Stuart or get to know him at all. *That's because he doesn't give a flaming flip who Lena marries.*

I'll bet he's afraid she's going to ask him to pay for the wedding. The thought of him cheaping out on Lena enraged me further.

"There's something else." Lena laced her fingers through Stuart's. "We've set a date. We're getting married on Sunday, August first."

My mind jumped back and forth between the possibilities. "You mean . . . next year?"

She shook her head. "This year. In seven weeks! On the beach!"

As I absorbed the news, she went on. "It'll be small. Stuart's parents and brothers will come here for the wedding, and you'll be there, Bree, and our friends. And Dad? I was hoping you'd come too. We won't exactly have an aisle that you can walk me down, but you could give me away."

Watching a sad combination of hope and resignation cross her face, I cursed our tiny and useless family. I glanced over at our father.

"Of course, I'll try to come," Dad was saying. "I should be able to reschedule appointments I have in the Midwest around that time. Topeka, Tulsa . . ."

Stuart and Lena regarded him in silence while my anger bubbled and boiled. What did he mean by "I'll try to come"? It didn't sound like much of a promise to me.

"There shouldn't be a conflict. The wedding's on a Sunday." I tried to speak calmly.

Lena had this uncertain, fluttery look that she got when she was gearing up for total emotional collapse. One glance at Stuart told me he saw it as well.

My dad, however, was oblivious. "Yes, but I have to travel Sunday to keep my work schedule on Monday." Bland and unapologetic as ever. "But as I said, I'll make every effort to reschedule."

My fighting instinct kicked it up to overdrive. "*Every effort?* Dad, it's her wedding!"

His lips drew down into a haughty expression. "And I said I would do my best! I have responsibilities to my clients."

Oh, please. The man sold Pap smear kits to gynecologists.

I exploded. "What makes it so impossible for you to be there for Lena?"

"Physician relations. Keeping them supplied so their practices run smoothly—"

"Seriously, Dad? Reorder supplies—that's your big emergency?" There were a dozen ways he could take care of his clients and still come to Lena's wedding. Was he really that stupid, or did he think I was?

A dull brick red infused his cheeks and neck. "You've never understood the responsibilities I have!"

I was on my feet, yelling. "I understand full well the responsibilities you had to be a father to me and Lena. Which you ignored!"

Stuart stood as well. "Bree," he said soothingly, "let's talk about this calmly, okay?"

"Let's not! Let's talk about how much Dad sucked as a father!"

Dad's eyes turned squinty and mean. "Let's talk about how you girls drove your mother out of the house with your constant bickering and disobedience! No wonder she never came back!"

My breath caught. I felt as if an iron fist had wrapped itself around my heart and squeezed it dry. Lena and I stared at each other, unable to comprehend that Dad could ever say anything so terrible to us, could ever *think* anything so terrible.

Lena started to cry, burying her face in Stuart's shoulder. In the meantime, the easygoing Stuart had gone white and was giving my dad a look of pure contempt.

I could see Dad withdraw into himself, the way he'd always done. He hadn't moved, but he was a million miles away. He'd probably spaced us all out and wasn't even conscious of Lena's distress, or my rage.

That made me even more furious. "Hey, earth to Dad!" I snapped my fingers in front of his face while he shifted his weight on the sofa and looked at the door, as if measuring the length of his escape route.

"What a despicable thing to say!" I hissed. "You made Lena cry!"

"You've made me cry, just as much as Dad!"

Lena was talking to *me*.

"I . . . what?" I couldn't believe it. "All I've done is stick up for you!" And yet, she was turning against me.

"I want us to all get along! For once in my life, at my wedding, I want my family all together and happy!" Lena blew her nose with a tissue that Stuart had handed to her. "Dad? Please come to my wedding? Please? And Bree? Please be nice to Dad? It's all I want from you two." She gazed pleadingly at Dad, who looked like he wished he were at the North Pole, maybe, or in an alligator-infested swamp—anywhere but here.

"Well, I'll do my part." I huffed. "But you heard what he said. He blamed us for Mom's leaving!"

Dad was actually putting on his jacket, as if leaving was the appropriate thing to do at this moment. Of course his mind was already on Mars or wherever it had escaped to. "Lena, I'm off. I'll stay in touch. Stuart, Sabrina, goodbye."

And with that, he was out the door. "Dad!" I called out, then stopped because he was gone. This was awful. I couldn't bear the way Stuart and Lena were looking at me. "Hey, I'm not the one who's bailing on you!"

"You weren't exactly helpful either." The statement came from Stuart, which made me feel even worse.

"You're just like him, you know!" Lena blew her nose, her cheeks streaked with tears.

It took a second before I realized she was still talking to me. "What? After all I've done for you all your life?"

"Of course, your giant sacrifices! I've heard about those too all my life! You're just like Dad. You guys think of no one but yourselves!"

"How can you say that?" My insides were crumbling from hurt feelings and betrayal.

Stuart put his arms around Lena. "Let's chill for now. Bree, maybe we'll see you in a couple of days?" In the nicest of ways, he was throwing me out.

"Okay." Stinging, I grabbed my bag and left.

Twenty-Six

The next day, the hours crawled by like doomed cars trapped in a never-ending rush hour. At long last, an email came in from Kaitlyn. Dread filled me as I opened it.

Sabrina,

Your photo is perfect—compelling and different! As for the red dress, I'm sure you'll find something else that's appropriate. Just think evening gown!

I must confess that I haven't been able to find a venue with a gorgeous staircase that meets all our other needs as well . . . and I have scoured Manhattan! So we may have to settle for a more run-of-the-mill entrance by doorway. No matter. We'll make it fabulous! I'm still considering having a dashing Count Richland accompany you to the party. However, I've not yet located a hot actor nephew or brother-in-law who's available for the job. Would you have any suggestions?

Speaking of fabulous, three more glowing reviews have come in (attached), and you're being considered for a book club selection. We're ecstatic here at Fast Track and so proud of you!

Best,

Kaitlyn

P.S. Only three more weeks! Aren't you excited?

I read it over twice, the first time in a state of total numbness, the second with growing joy. She didn't care how much I weighed! I didn't have to be thin and beautiful. Of course, the glowing reviews and interest from book clubs hadn't hurt a bit.

Hah! Maybe I *was* good enough! Maybe I *could* write, after all. And maybe, just maybe, my weight wasn't the one thing in the entire world that mattered. I couldn't believe I had suffered so much over this for so long. What a waste of time. *Remember this.* I had better things to do than jump hurdles that existed only in my own mind.

And yet, visions of cheeseburgers continued to dance in my head. Visions of milkshakes, York Peppermint Patties, french fries, potato chips, barbecued ribs.

You would think that, having dodged the giant bullet of Kaitlyn's wrath, I would be happy. Yet how could I not want to eat after the fiasco of Monday night? I'd disappointed the most important person in my life, my little sister, and the weird thing was that I knew I was completely in the right. Dad was a jerk. Lena was wasting her time on him. So, obviously, she should be the one to call me, right, to take the first step?

I waited.

On Tuesday, following Michelle's suggestion, I took a photo of the "Make a Friend" list at my program meeting. It was a sign-up sheet passed around at every meeting; members wrote their names and phone numbers on it if they were willing to receive out-reach calls.

That night, I picked out eight phone numbers belonging to people who I'd spoken to at least once (and who would remember me), leaving messages for six of them. "Hi, this is Sabrina from program. Just reaching out because I really want to eat something, and if I'm talking on the phone, I can't eat! Well, technically, I *can* eat, but I wouldn't. Call back if you want to, but no obligation."

Just the act of calling and leaving messages helped. In two cases, I found my victims at home and talked to them, which also helped. The other six people called me back, some immediately and others within a day or so. But nothing from Lena.

On top of all that, no text from Daniel. I comforted myself with the thought that he might have a good excuse, like maybe he'd had an aneurysm or was lying trapped somewhere under a heavy object. It made me feel better.

As Wednesday went by, any serenity that I had left crumbled away. More than anything, I wanted to binge. I wanted to lock myself into my apartment and eat myself sick. I would eventually wander off somewhere and disappear, and they would find my body at the bottom of a canyon, half consumed by beetles and coyotes. Then they'd be sorry.

One day at a time, I told myself. It was more like one moment at a time. But I sucked it up and stuck to my food plan of three meals and two snacks a day.

Thursday came, and I needed Lena. I didn't care anymore who was right, and just wanted her to reach out to me. But I still couldn't bring myself to call her, so on Friday, I did the next best thing and called Stuart. I hadn't seen or talked to him since that awful night with Dad.

He greeted me with, "Hey, girl, we miss you."

"I miss you too!" I wailed, bursting into tears.

"Come over tonight. Lena'll be out working, but I'll show you how to wax your board."

That day, I drowned myself in my work. As the eve of the *Circus Murders* party grew closer, I had decided things were in pretty good shape. I had a solution for every potential problem, a backup plan for every emergency, a line on replacements for every person who fell ill or piece of equipment that broke down. The only thing I didn't have was just the right person to cover the party for me while I was in New York. Although Josh would return for the event, I knew he couldn't be the Sabrina clone I needed. Josh would circulate, slap backs, and exchange boisterous greetings, but he could never keep this thing running smoothly. Also, there was the eentsy-weentsy problem that he didn't yet know I planned to be absent.

At six o'clock that evening, I knocked on Lena and Stuart's door. A babbling Lena was spinning through the apartment, gathering up her things to leave. She didn't quite look at me, nor I at her. "I'm working a cocktail reception for Olivia. Her kid broke his arm this afternoon, so she's going to be late. So *I'm* in charge of the setup!" Lena sounded as if she could hardly believe it. "I *have* to get it right. I'm getting there an hour early, just to be sure."

"You got this, babe." Stuart was a model of calm confidence. "Do you have the checklists we made?"

She nodded, patting a file folder she was holding. "Wish me luck! I'll call you if I need you."

As she whirled out the door, I gave Stuart a skeptical eye. "Since when do you know anything about catering?"

"I don't, really. I'm just giving moral support." He took a couple of surfboards down from their wall racks and laid them out on the living room floor.

I'd figured as much. As far as I knew, Stuart was your basic trust fund baby. I tried to imagine what his life had been like growing up—the parties, vacations, trips to Europe. Something—I didn't know what—had brought him down to his current lowly status. Drugs, maybe, or just getting his way one too many times.

"Using the corner of a square of wax, make diagonal lines, like so." He demonstrated, kneeling beside one of the boards. I took the other one, copying him. We worked side by side for a time, peacefully crosshatching the boards with lines of wax while Stuart took Lena's calls.

Every fifteen minutes or so, his phone would ring, with Lena's voice shrill and panicky at the other end. I was used to Lena's ditziness. Stuart was the shocker. "Hon, slow down," he would say, offering calm, reassuring advice and ending with, "No problem, babe."

A server called to say she was marooned by the side of the road with a flat tire. Stuart arranged for road service to come and change it. Another server cut herself on the vegetable slicer. With supplies from a first aid kit that he'd put in the trunk of Lena's car, Stuart talked them through sanitizing and bandaging the injured finger.

Their cream cheese was past its expiration date and smelled off, but they couldn't spare someone for the time it would take to drive to a store to replace it. It was Stuart who remembered that Olivia was coming to the party from her son's hospital and could easily stop to pick some up along the way. The food tables had been placed in an inconvenient, dead-end corner. Stuart looked over a copy of the party layout, spoke with the host, and suggested a new location that made the food display both attractive and easy to reach.

"Olivia should be paying *you*!" I told my future brother-in-law. He sure knew how to troubleshoot. Exactly the sort of person I needed for the *Circus Murders* party.

Wait a minute. I shook my head, trying to clear it.

I was clearly delusional.

After all, this was Boomer.

Lena's calls to Stuart had stopped, indicating that Olivia had arrived at the party. Stuart put on a classic rock station, to which we peacefully completed the waxing of his board collection and then sprawled in the armchairs, drinking cranberry juice.

"Lena sure needed a lot of help tonight," I said, stating the obvious.

"Yeah," Stuart said. He looked over and exchanged a glance with me, one which said, *We both know she's a little wacky, but we really love her.* "She'll be okay. She just needs to build up her self-confidence."

My throat ached a little, seeing how simply and totally he accepted her for who she was. "What did you do before you came out to California?"

"Worked. Every summer during high school and college and for three years after college."

I had somehow imagined him bumming change on a street corner. "You're kidding! What kind of jobs did you have?"

"You name it. Washed dishes, waited tables, stocked shelves. Parked cars, worked retail, worked as a bouncer and a security guard. Those were the summer jobs. Then, after college, I went through a management training program with our family company. Mainly just to make them happy."

"Why'd you leave? It sounds like a good job."

"Needed to bust loose. I'd spent my whole life doing what my dad wanted me to do. It didn't go over too well with the rents, as you can guess."

"So what's next? Teaching surfing?"

"Nope! Actually, I'm looking around for the right thing."

Impulsively, I spoke, knowing I was making the right decision. "Do you want to make some extra money for a couple days' work?"

"Maybe. What is it?"

I told him.

Twenty-Seven

A text came in: *Bree, I've swung a brief trip back to LA. Would you like to meet up tomorrow night? Hoping to see you.*

My heart palpitated. Daniel was hoping to see me.

Would I like to meet up with him tomorrow night?

Would I like to eat a hot fudge sundae? Go to Paris? Win the lottery?

On the other hand, I was a little mad at him for only texting me four times in the three weeks he'd been gone. Maybe I should play hard to get.

I'm free. What did you have in mind?

I dunno. What would you like to do?

How about something involving you, me, and that hot fudge sundae? No? Too obvious?

How about a walk on the beach, then dinner?

Sold.

We stood without speaking on the sand at the edge of the water. We had found a place for our shoes and rolled up our pant legs. Daniel had brought a blanket too, which he folded and tucked underneath his arm. Since it was a Thursday evening, the bike and walking paths were still full, but the sunbathers had left and only a few people were down by us, near the ocean.

My head spun at the thought that Daniel was right here, standing next to me, that I could reach out and touch him if I wanted to. And I did want to.

The red sun dipped toward the horizon, creating a flaming backdrop for the latticework of steel beams that formed the Ferris wheel at the pier. "I love red sunsets," I told Daniel. "Too bad they're caused by air pollution."

He laughed. "You're funny." And then he took my hand and did that thing where he intertwined his fingers with mine, thereby throwing me into a swoon. "Let's walk," he said.

"Okay."

He could have said, "Let's walk naked down Hollywood Boulevard," and I still would have said, "Okay."

I thought of Kaitlyn's suggestion that I find my own Count-Richland-lookalike date for the party. Would Daniel want to come?

I asked him. "Kaitlyn, my editor, said they'd cover your travel and hotel."

Sizzling eye contact. "That sounds awesome," he said. "But I don't know if I can get away from work. I can't say yes or no until the last minute."

"That's all right."

We walked on, swinging our hands forward and back. "So you'd like me to come see you in New York, huh?" That great smile, now teasing me.

I shrugged, looking up at him through my eyelashes. "Job requirement." More eye contact.

He shook his head. "You really make a guy work for it, you know."

"I do?" I asked, thrilled by the turn the conversation had taken.

"Yeah, I mean, here I've been sweating it out for weeks, trying to get your attention, and you've been, like, whatever."

Was that really how it had seemed to him? "But I've barely heard from you since you started this new case!"

He stopped walking, looking crestfallen. "I texted you a lot in the beginning!"

He *had* tried to reach me! "I don't think I got them."

He thought about it. "I know the Wi-Fi wasn't that great. And then I stopped texting as much when I didn't hear from you."

"I'm sorry you thought I wasn't answering you."

"It's okay."

He spread the blanket out on the sand, and we sat down. Daniel wasted no time reaching for me. And then I found myself doing the most fun thing I've ever done in my entire life: lying on a beach at sunset making out with a guy I was crazy about. We lay together on the blanket, the sounds of our breathing mixed with the crashing waves of the Pacific, the smell of salt and kelp and peppermint Tic Tacs, and the sensation of gritty sand and, best of all, his lips, his tongue, his hands against my skin.

As dreamy as Daniel was, I had committed myself ahead of time to a PG-13 evening. I didn't want to have any regrets afterward. We eventually disentangled ourselves, struggled back up to the parking lot, and found a little seafood dive, where we sat side by side out-doors at a picnic table, thighs touching, eating huge naked shrimp with cocktail sauce.

Daniel ordered a Corona, which we shared, drinking out of the same glass, leaning against each other. He asked me about the book I was writing and laughed at my stories about Josh and our crazy showbiz clients.

Once again, I felt like a full-fledged member of the world community. Not just an undeserving bystander looking in from the outside, living a half-life, but a person who loved, who was loved, who took part and received and gave back.

A person who belonged.

Twenty-Eight

Stuart and I spent the next couple of days at my office going over every detail of the party. He delighted in all the fun parts—the costumes, the performing dogs, the cotton candy, the big top tent. At the same time, he was quick to adapt to my system of checklists and contingency plans. I knew he was taking it all seriously, the security for celebrities, the safety equipment and procedures necessary to protect both the performers and the guests. At one point, a call came in. "Luckily, this is a minor problem," I told Stuart. "The guy playing the ringmaster just got a job on a cruise ship. He was more window dressing than anything, so I don't think we'll need to replace him. We'll just return his costume."

"What if I wore it?" Stuart asked. "I mean, it kind of goes with my job description, don't you think?"

It *did* kind of go with his job description, not to mention that Stuart the Ringmaster would make a nice additional piece of eye candy for my already visually exciting party.

"Check our costume order," I said, "and make sure you get one in the right size."

It also turned out that Stuart was a fan of Buck Billingsley's. "This rocks!" he told me. "I'm going to meet him?"

"Not only will you meet him, but you'll have to keep him happy." I handed him a list of things that we'd learned to have on hand when Buck was around, starting with heating pads and ibuprofen and ending with Chivas Regal Scotch Whisky.

While getting Stuart up to speed on the party turned out to be pretty straightforward, telling Josh was a bit trickier, particularly because he chose to return to the office from Texas without warning. His appearance startled me. He was pale, with deep circles under his eyes, and noticeably thinner. He'd picked up a hacking cough, yet he had an energy in his voice, I was glad to notice, that I hadn't heard in a long time.

Despite his appearance, I knew he was happy about Corinne, who was doing much better with a new treatment they'd found for her. She had new meds that she was taking regularly, and she was no longer hearing voices.

Josh rolled into the office to find Stuart half-dressed in his ring-master costume, while I tested the cotton candy machine, ribbons of pink flying through the air, sticking to mirrors and aquarium glass.

"Josh!" I threw him a carefully casual smile, my hands encrusted in pink sugar, while trying to get Stuart's attention. Looking like a classic romance novel protagonist, Stuart made a striking impression, his back to the room, blond hair down around his shoulders, long lean legs in tan breeches tucked into black leather knee-high boots. A snowy white shirt, not yet buttoned, exposed his tan chest from multiple angles in the many wall mirrors. He scowled as he concentrated on buttoning his cuff links.

"This is Stuart Livingston." As I made the introduction, I saw a speculative look come into Josh's eyes, the look of a Hollywood talent agent who is ticking through the checkboxes. Looks: check. Height: check. Leading man potential: check.

"Where are his headshots?" Josh asked me.

"Oh, Josh, no—"

"No?" Josh frowned. I could see him thinking: what kind of amateur was this, who didn't even have headshots? "I'd like to see him cut his hair," he told me, speaking as if Stuart were a piece of furniture.

Stuart did a startled double take. "Cut my . . . ?"

"Great physique. Just right for . . ." Josh nodded to me sagely. I knew he meant nude scenes.

Better to redirect this conversation. "Josh, Stuart isn't an actor!"

Another frown. "What's he doing here then?"

I tried to answer, but Stuart was clearly tired of being treated like an overstuffed chair. "I'm going to supervise the *Circus Murders* party on Saturday night while Sabrina's in New York."

Utter silence. I didn't dare look at Josh. Finally, I squinted an eye in his direction.

In a dangerously quiet voice, Josh said, "New York?"

"Yep," said the oblivious Stuart. "Her book's coming out that day."

"Your *book*?" Josh went white. "You wrote a book?" Now red was creeping up from his collar. "You signed a nondisclosure agreement!"

It took me a moment to realize what he was thinking. Then I had to swallow my laughter. "You think I wrote a tell-all? About you? And your clients?"

The red now verged toward purple. "I'll sue you for everything you've got!"

Like anyone would ever read a book about Josh and his roster of C-listers. I couldn't allow myself to laugh, because it would hurt his feelings. "I would never do that."

"Then . . . what . . . ?"

"I guess I need to fill you in. Josh, do you mind if we all sit down in your office? You too, Stuart." I owed this to Josh.

So I told him everything. "I've probably written a dozen novels, but now one has been accepted for publication. It's a romance, coming out on the seventeenth."

To my surprise, a faint interest stirred in his eyes. "Corinne loves romances. Will you comp me one?"

"Of course." An actual friend would have bought one, not asked for a freebie. "Anyway, the party's totally covered. Stuart's an executive with Livingston Textiles," I told Josh, figuring it might be true someday, "and he knows everything cold. He'll oversee what I put into place."

He would too. Little Boomer had grown up, and I trusted him.

After Josh and I saw Stuart off, we sat back down in his office. I shifted my position in my chair, crossed my legs, uncrossed them, then recrossed them in the other direction. Something had changed in Josh's absence.

For one thing, I'd more or less done his job in that time. At least, I had as far as Alexa Fredericks went, because I'd had no choice. "Did you look at the Fredericks contract yet?"

"Haven't had time. I sure hope you didn't give the store away." Josh was reverting to his habitual grumpiness, and I was already tired of it.

"No, I got exactly the terms you wanted. Except for *Dead by Midnight.* I had to include it."

"I wanted to negotiate that separately! I could've gotten ten thousand for it!"

"Yeah, well, she wouldn't sign without it. And I got twelve thousand for it." *Take that, chump.* I crossed my legs and arms and scowled at him.

Silence. I could practically feel steam rising from my forehead. This was it. I was not going back to the same old job with the same old Josh.

Because I wasn't the same old Sabrina.

I finally spoke. "I think the appropriate words would be, 'Thank you, Sabrina.' You could also acknowledge the fact that I kept your business alive for almost two months and brought in a valuable new client you probably would have lost without me." I stood and began a majestic exit from the office.

"Sabrina, wait!" Josh actually put out a hand to stop me. "Okay! You're right." He coughed and cleared his throat, as if it pained him to say something nice. "Thank you. You saved my ass."

I just looked at him. "Anything else?"

He assumed an innocent air. "Like what?"

"A signing bonus. For bringing in Alexa."

A howl of anguish. "What? Are you kidding?"

"You heard me."

He pounded his chest with a fist. "You're giving me a heart attack!"

"Good thing you've got all those doctors on hand."

It went on for some time, but I could not be swayed. Eventually, we struck a deal.

Twenty-Nine

Now if I could just work things out with Lena. We still hadn't spoken since our blowup, although I knew we both wanted to. Increasingly, I found it hard to justify my own behavior.

I talked to Michelle about it. "I mean, the weird thing is, I know I'm right. My dad's a giant asshole and doesn't deserve to be forgiven. And yet that doesn't seem to matter. What's the point of being right if I make both my sister and myself miserable? And what's it to me if he's in Lena's wedding? It's her wedding, and she should have anyone she wants."

Michelle was silent for a moment as she considered what I'd said. "Holding grudges can be hard work."

"No kidding."

So I called Lena and asked if I could come over. It took us two minutes to make up when I arrived. "I'm so sorry," I told my sister, falling into her arms. "I was an idiot. I'll be nice to Dad." And I called my father and apologized. "I don't want that to stand between you and Lena. We'd both love for you to attend her wedding."

He didn't say much, and Lena didn't really know where she stood on the wedding, but I'd done what I could. I'd made amends.

Daniel had taken off again for Miami, and there was no set date for his return. Things were different, though, since our night on the beach. We texted every other day, just quick notes checking in, and FaceTimed a couple of times a week, right before bed.

I loved FaceTiming because I could see Daniel, really take him in, with that sexy dark shadow on his cheeks and those blue eyes and that face that was so handsome and expressive. In Florida, it was late when he called, usually around eleven, so he'd be in bed, propped up against the bed pillows, wearing an old T-shirt, his iPad in his lap or on his knees.

I also hated FaceTiming because he could really see me, all of me, which seemed unfortunate. Lena and Stuart had always insisted I was pretty, but I just couldn't believe it. All I saw was my hair collapsed from the day, my chubby arms, my face pale from a total lack of makeup. I didn't want Daniel to see any of that; it was just too embarrassing.

We tried to keep our talks short because we had long workdays ahead of us, but they nevertheless seemed to run on until midnight, or even one o'clock, Florida time, until Daniel was yawning uncontrollably and saying, "Don't let me stay up this late again." But then, inevitably, he would end up doing it again. Talking with him at night, in the dark, from our respective beds created a delicious sense of intimacy that we both hated to end.

"Any chance you could come to Florida one of these weekends?" he asked me one evening.

I gasped. "I would *love* to! I wish I could."

"Why can't you? Is it the money? I'll pay for it."

"Thanks. That's really sweet," I said, thrilled that he would offer something like that.

"So, will you come?"

I hesitated. "Where would I stay?"

"I'll get you your own room, if that's what's bothering you. I wouldn't, you know, pressure you . . ."

"I know." That wasn't the problem. The problem was that I was still at least thirty pounds overweight. The thought of facing Daniel like that without clothing or a space blanket or some other form of protective shield was simply not possible.

Time to calculate. If I could lose three pounds a week, I'd be at goal weight in . . .

"Ten weeks."

"What?"

"Ten weeks. I can come visit you in ten weeks."

"Ten weeks! That's two and a half months from now!"

"Well, I won't be ready until then."

Daniel was silent, his brow crumpled, probably trying to work out what I could possibly be thinking. Finally, he asked, "Ready for what?"

I squirmed. "Ready for . . . you know."

He sighed. "I'm too tired for guessing games. Out with it, Bree."

"Well, you know. If we decided to . . . to . . . take our relationship to a more intimate level?"

"As in, getting naked?"

"That's one way to put it."

Daniel looked torn between amazement and hilarity. "So, let me get this straight. You're not ready to get naked this weekend, but you will be ten weeks from now?"

"Yes."

"Not nine weeks from now? Or eleven weeks from now? Ten weeks?"

I drew myself up with as much dignity as I could muster. "Don't make fun of me."

"I'm sorry, but I don't understand. In ten weeks . . . what? You'll know me better? Well enough to take off your clothes? What's so special about ten weeks?"

"I'll be thinner!"

"So?" Daniel looked genuinely confused.

"So I'll be more attractive to you!"

His jaw dropped. "You think you're not attractive to me now, that you have to lose weight for me to find you desirable?"

"Yes."

He shook his head. "You are so wrong."

"*Really?*" I allowed myself to be delighted for a moment, until I realized that he was just being nice. "I don't believe you."

"You don't believe me?" His face reddened. "You honestly think I don't want you?"

"Well," I said in a small voice. "I guess I *kind of* think you want me. But I think you'll want me *more* if I lose weight."

He ran his hands through his hair so it stood up in little spikes, and his face reddened even more. "Sabrina, you are a gorgeous and totally fuckable woman *right now*! Can I be any clearer?"

"*Really?*" My heart rejoiced. Daniel thought I was totally fuckable!

"Really," he said. "And, if you'd like, next time I see you, I'll prove it to you." More eye contact, now revved up to the temperature of molten lava.

"Now, look, I'm exhausted and I've got a bitch of a day tomorrow, so I'm going to say good night. You okay?" he asked.

"Yes."

"Okay then." A long look that warmed me to my toes. "Good night, Bree."

"Good night, Daniel."

After the line went dead, I lay there levitating a few inches above the mattress and repeating to myself: *gorgeous and totally fuckable.* That's what Daniel thought of me. It was hard to get much better than that.

I turned over, letting the words wash over me, feeling beautiful. Then it occurred to me that Daniel hadn't actually *seen* me naked, that the gorgeous and totally fuckable Sabrina he referred to was really just a figment of his imagination. My levitating body plopped back onto the mattress.

Don't spoil this moment, Sabrina. Just take him at his word. Believe him.

But that's the problem, I thought, as I turned over again, trying to get comfortable.

I just couldn't quite believe him.

Thirty

Saturday morning, July 17, and reveling in my first morning as a real, live published author. Up at seven, splurging on toast and poached eggs from room service in my Manhattan hotel room while I looked over my agenda for the day. A tour of the Fast Track offices in the morning, two bookstore signings, and finally, from six to eight, the party that had been the source of so much mental agony.

For the hundredth time, I thanked my higher power up above who'd given me a sister with a special talent for dressing chubby people. I gave thanks for the slimming linen pantsuit that I hoped would make me look crisp and cool all day, just as a pillar of the literary establishment should look. I twisted my hair back in a gold barrette, put on lip gloss, and gathered a few personal effects in a thin leather briefcase as I got ready to meet Kaitlyn at the Fast Track offices.

When my cell phone rang, surprising me with Daniel's name on the display screen, I fell on it. "You just caught me," I said. "I'm leaving to meet my editor."

"Really? Well, this is kind of short notice, but good news! I was able to pull a few strings today, so if your invitation's still open, I can get up there tonight for your party!"

"Omigod, that's fantastic!" My day had suddenly gone from an A plus to an A quadruple plus. "It's a dressy party, though, so can you wear a suit?"

"Sure. I'll pick you up at your hotel room."

"I can't wait to see you!"

"Oh, and I'll get my own room," he added. "Didn't want you to think I'd forgotten the ten-week rule."

"I didn't. Thanks."

Daniel was coming to New York! I allowed myself a moment of total happiness.

But business first. It was time to meet Kaitlyn Mann.

As I walked into the Fast Track offices, my eyes passed over a ficus tree, shelves displaying books in colorful jackets, and a large model airplane hanging in the corner. A short woman with a large, round posterior stood arranging piles of books on a table that was part of a prominently positioned display. For my book.

My eyes misted over. My name in large letters, the voluptuous melon-breasted Cecily, a chestnut stallion prancing and tossing his head—Fast Track had made beautifully rendered illustrations produced in life-size cutouts. Above it all, the title, *The Passion of Cecily*, in gold script.

On the table, the woman had placed a pile of my books with several pens beside them. I would be signing a bunch of them, I now remembered, to leave with the publisher. I'd dreamed about this; I could hardly believe it was really happening. I tried pinching myself, remembering that's what you're supposed to do in these situations, but I couldn't say I found it particularly helpful.

"Exciting, isn't it?" the woman said to me. She was probably in her fifties, with blondish hair pulled back into a messy bun. Dressed in earth tones—a cowl-necked long-sleeved sweater, ankle-length flowing skirt—accented by half a dozen big pieces of Native American turquoise and silver jewelry. Soft, suede ankle boots finished the look.

Were those chopsticks holding her hair in place?

"*So* exciting!" I held out my hand. "I'm Sabrina Hunter, here to see Kaitlyn Mann."

Her eyes twinkled. "I know!"

The voice was so familiar. I gasped as the realization hit me. "Kaitlyn?"

"None other!"

They *were* chopsticks. Red lacquer. The cheerleader look was long gone. Apparently, I wasn't the only one who used out-of-date pictures.

"Wow! It's so good to meet you!"

"The feeling is mutual. You look perfect!" she announced. She handed me a folder of crucial information I would need for my day. *Just like I'd always done for Josh.*

It felt like a sign. Maybe this was it. The baton was being passed.

As I took the elevator up to my hotel room, I looked back on my first day as a real published author on a real paid-for-by-the-publisher book tour. I had a satisfying pain in my hand from the seventy-five or so books I'd signed (sixty-two for the customers who'd attended the book signing events and the rest for book shop owners to sell afterward). The really good news, according to Kaitlyn, was the large number of preorders and enthusiastic reviews that continued to come in, all good omens for future sales.

The people at the bookstore signings had been awesome, listening attentively to my ten-minute reading and asking lots of questions. It felt incredible, after spending years alone with my book, to share it with others, to see how it affected them. The fact that people responded and related to my book moved me unexpectedly. I arrived back at my hotel room elated and feeling incredibly lucky.

Now, I had a mere hour before Daniel was going to show up—a single hour to primp myself into a state of total fabulousness. I went to work. I bathed, shaved, tweezed, exfoliated, moisturized, brushed, flossed, and scented, then finally slipped into what I considered to be Lena's finest accomplishment as a personal shopper: a long, simple, stunningly shimmery dress with a boat neck and a slit up the side that went to mid-thigh.

The dress was gold. Against my dark hair, brushed long and straight, even I had to say it was beautiful. And I felt beautiful too.

A knock at the door. My heart hammering in my chest, I opened it.

Daniel stood there, darkly handsome and masculine in a charcoal-gray wool suit. His mouth opened at the sight of me. "Wow."

"Really? Wow?" I stepped back to let him in, feeling shy.

"You look amazing." He ran his eyes over me, openly admiring me, then took my arm. "You all ready, Miss Published Author? How'd things go today?" And he swept me out into the night while I told him everything.

The absence of a splendid staircase and stunning authoress in a fabulous red evening gown had taken the steam out of Kaitlyn's grandiose dreams for my party. It wasn't hard to nix her next suggestion: that I make an entrance astride a prancing chestnut stallion. To my huge relief, the party in the end was a much more stripped-down event involving Kaitlyn ushering Daniel and me around and introducing us to people whose names I probably should have recognized but didn't.

And it didn't matter. "Let's not eat a lot at the party," Daniel had suggested in my ear. "I know a great Italian place for dinner."

"That sounds perfect."

I continued to live the dream. In so doing, I discovered a couple of things about myself that I had never thought of in my whole twenty-seven years on earth.

First, I had never before been the center of attention. It would clearly be impossible in a family with parents who abandoned and ignored you and a sister four years younger than you. At school, my sister grabbed the attention spot, because she was always the one in trouble. In college, it was my outgoing life-of-the-party boyfriend who snagged the invitations to games and other events, while I served as the invisible plus-one.

Fast Track's party was the first occasion in my life where I found myself featured under a persistent and powerful spotlight.

The second thing I discovered was that I didn't really like being the center of attention. It meant I had to talk to people all the time and smile at them, which made me feel tired and shy and awkward. I couldn't use any of my usual crowd survival techniques, like hiding in the bathroom with the door locked. At one point, Daniel found me in a dark corner stress-eating guacamole and had to gently talk me back into circulation.

I did like seeing large piles of my book, with its racy, eye-catching cover, and watching people snatch up their copies and buy them. And most of all, I liked walking around with Daniel, his arm around my waist, introducing him to people, just as if he were really mine. Having two such incredible things happen on the same night—publication of my first book and a special date with a very special guy—those things I liked a lot.

By eight o'clock, most of the crowd had gone. Kaitlyn found me to apologize for being unable to take me out to dinner. "I'm flying to Chicago at six A.M. tomorrow for a conference," she told me, "but I'm thinking you may have other plans anyway." She cast a quizzical look and a smile in Daniel's direction.

"Yeah, I'm fine," I told her, unable to prevent a sigh of total bliss. "Don't worry about me."

"We have reservations," Daniel said in my ear, delighting me even further. We hailed a cab and traveled to a small Italian restaurant with dim light and candles, where we consumed scrumptious sips and bites of wines and cheeses and pastas and lovely things with names I couldn't pronounce.

We talked about the night we first met, when Michelle had introduced us at the meeting at All Saints' Church.

"I saw you come in," I told Daniel. "You sat in the front row." I didn't mention how I had lusted after him throughout the meeting and, by the end, had decided to become the mother of his children.

"I noticed you too," he said. "I was pretty sure you were new, so I headed over right off the bat to give you the new membership package."

"That was diligent of you."

"Not really." When I looked at him in surprise, he added, "I just . . . had a feeling I wanted to get to know you."

Insides feeling warm and fuzzy. Legs like limp spaghetti. "You wanted to get to know me?"

"Yeah. I definitely did," he said.

"I wanted to get to know you too."

"Will there be anything else?" The waiter stood over our table.

Daniel and I spoke together. "The check."

"Do you want to walk home?" he asked me.

"Do you know where we are?"

"Sure do." He led the way, pointing things out as we went. Our restaurant was on a small street in the West Village. We walked in a companionable silence toward Washington Square, enjoying the night air and the chance to stretch our legs.

Occasionally, we would slow down to admire an unusually lovely building façade or to skirt a patch of broken concrete—both occurrences equally likely in New York.

Music reached our ears. On the stoop of a brownstone, four musicians with flutes and oboes played an impromptu concert for passersby. We stopped for a moment to listen.

As we reached the front doors of my hotel, Daniel drew me close and kissed me. "This was a great night," he said, smiling down at me. "Thanks for inviting me."

"You're welcome. Having you here made it so much better."

His eyes grew warm and crinkly around the corners. "Really? I like hearing that."

I tightened my arms around him. "Stay the night with me."

"Whoa! That's a pretty big change of heart." Half-teasing, half-serious.

"I can't help it. You're too hard to resist."

"What about the ten weeks?"

"I changed my mind."

"Are you sure?"

I pursed my lips as I considered his question. "I'll turn the lights off."

He threw back his head and laughed. "Oh, no, you won't!"

Two bicycles whizzed by, narrowly missing a taxi, who blared his horn at them. Laughter and conversation drifted back from the bicyclists as they proceeded down the street, if anything, picking up speed.

The balmy night air brushed my face, and the lights of the city sparkled.

As the doorman let us in, I once again had that rare feeling that I was entitled to all of it, deserving of my place in the world, and to all that life had to offer. I was ready to stake my claim to joy.

I was worthy of love.

Four Weeks Later . . .

Dear God,

I'm still not sure why I should write you a letter, since you already know everything and probably control everything too. Maybe it's for my own benefit, because I find that ideas, when they're forced through my fingers onto a keyboard, line up for me in a way that they just don't otherwise.

First, I'll never let anyone try to tell me that fulfilling a dream can disappoint me or leave me feeling empty. I am officially now a best-selling author, so I'm living my dream. And you know what? It ROCKS!

With the royalties I'm making, I'll be able to pay off my advance and my student loans—just barely, but still! And Fast Track has bought the next two books in my series, so more advance money will be coming in. Josh is being really nice to me, because he wants me to keep working for him, but Stuart, who's taking a finance class, is helping me run the numbers to see if (when) I can afford to quit.

Sad to say, my father bugged out on Lena's wedding. Never have I been so sorry to be right about something. But Stuart's family was incredibly nice to both me and Lena. They're thrilled about the change in Stuart, for which they give Lena all the credit. Stuart's dad and I gave Lena away, and I've never seen her happier.

I have a man in my life too, a wonderful, sexy, interesting, kind man with a sense of humor and a job! For my twenty-eighth birthday, he took me up to Lake Arrowhead for three blissful days. I haven't said this aloud, but I think I love him. I knew it from the first time we met but never told anyone or even dared to say it to myself. But I knew he was the one for me, and it turns out that he also knew I was the one for him.

As for my weight, I've lost some, but I couldn't tell you how much. I haven't weighed myself in a couple of months. Somehow, I've learned that the ideal of being super thin is just a carrot we hold out for ourselves, when the things we really want are love, friendship, laughter, a sense of purpose.

Although I know I've lost some of the weight, I don't really care, so long as all my clothes fit me comfortably. In fact, right now, my whole life fits me comfortably.

So God, whoever you are, wherever you are, thanks for everything. I'm happy.

Best always,

Sabrina

THE END

About Anne

Anne Pfeffer lives in Los Angeles, California, which she uses as the location for all her books. During her multifaceted career as a banker, then attorney, then finally, a novelist, she has liked being a novelist best. She tries to write stories that are fun and entertaining, in which the characters grow up or learn something important about themselves or the world. She is grateful to all the people who have read her books and written reviews to spread the word!

Connect with Anne

annepfefferbooks.com

Twitter.com/AnnePfeffer1

anne@annepfefferbooks.com

Leave a Review

If you enjoyed reading *Binge*, will you please take a moment to leave a review on your platform of choice? Reviews help self-published authors find more readers like you.

Made in the USA
Middletown, DE
15 February 2022